Despite [illegible] she was attracted to him

She was infuriated by his attitude, she hated him for disturbing her sleep, and she couldn't admire anyone who gave up his goals in order to waste away the rest of his life—yet Patty couldn't still her heart when Mike was around. It had to be his looks, she decided. She'd always been attracted to handsome men, and they'd always turned out to be idiots. At least with this one she knew he was an idiot from the start!

If she had Mike's talent she'd be using it. Not that owning a business was all that bad; it was the *kind* of business. What sort of adult wanted to spend all his time in a bar listening to teenage rock music?

An idiot, that was who.

But a damn sexy one.

BEVERLY SOMMERS
is also the author
of these titles in
Love Affair

CITY LIFE, CITY LOVE
UNSCHEDULED LOVE
VERDICT OF LOVE
THE LAST KEY
MIX AND MATCH
CHANGING PLACES
CONVICTIONS

Snowbird

BEVERLY SOMMERS

A Love Affair from

HARLEQUIN

London · Toronto · New York · Sydney

First published in Great Britain in 1987 by
Harlequin, 15–16 Brook's Mews, London W1A 1DR

ISBN 0 373 50599 X

18–0587

Printed and bound in Great Britain by
Cox & Wyman Ltd., Reading

Chapter One

It was the kind of day that made transplanted Northerners happy they had moved, Mike was thinking as he sat out on the front porch of the Honkytonk and watched all the tourists walk down Duval Street. Well, not exactly all the tourists: He somehow managed to miss the masculine variety.

He was watching one particular snowbird with a lot of blond hair and legs that looked a good five feet long and as a result almost missed seeing the taxi pull up in front and a passenger get out.

When he did finally notice, he couldn't believe his eyes. "Do you see what I see?" he asked Bobby Knuckles, who was seated beside him.

"I see." Knuckles, a baby face atop three hundred pounds of solid muscle, was squinting his eyes for a better look.

"Do you believe it?"

Knuckles blinked a couple of times. "Nope."

The woman getting out of the taxi was wearing a long cape that looked as though it had been made from a blanket, the hood of the cape pulled low over her face; long pants; high boots; and, as a final ludicrous touch, a red muffler wrapped around her neck. This when the temperature was 86 degrees Fahrenheit. In the shade. She lifted four suitcases out of the taxi.

"A nut case," observed Mike, deciding it was time for his first drink of the day. "An authentic loony-tune."

"Well," said Knuckles, "I've heard about Arabs who live in the desert and bundle up like that."

"This isn't the desert and she doesn't look like an Arab. At least what I can see of her. What the hell's she doing with four suitcases? She think there's a hotel in the alley?"

"She's gotta be going to Captain Harry's," said Knuckles. "She's probably with the band back there, got her equipment in the bags."

"You really believe that?" asked Mike.

"You got any better ideas?"

Mike watched as the woman tried to lift all four suitcases at once. She almost, but not quite, succeeded. Nudging Knuckles with his elbow, he said, "Give the lady a hand. And while you're at it, try to find out what her story is."

Knuckles gave him a look that said "You've got to be kidding," then seeing that Mike wasn't, got reluctantly to his feet. "Helping chicks with suitcases ain't my style," he complained.

"When was it ever said you had style?"

Mike had counted three more blondes and downed his first shot of tequila when Knuckles returned, a put-upon look on his face. He took his seat beside Mike again, after ordering a beer from Judy, who was tending bar, then leaned back on the stool and hooked one foot around the railing of the porch.

"Well?" asked Mike, getting exasperated by the wait.

"Didn't say a word, but she tipped me."

"Tipped you?"

"Yeah. Gave me fifty cents."

"You might make out better working for her. Where was she going?"

"This you won't believe, Mike. She's rented the apartment next door—the one over the Atari place."

"You're kidding."

"I kid you not."

"She's in for a big surprise."

"Yeah."

"I wouldn't have figured her the type for this neighborhood." Actually, in the fifteen years he had been there, he couldn't remember a female ever living in the alley.

"She's not the type for Key West, period."

Mike had to agree. No one who dressed like that was a sun lover. "Didn't you ask her anything?"

"I tried to be friendly, but every time I tried she lifted one of her eyebrows and gave me the same kind of look schoolteachers used to give me when I belched in school."

"You really don't have any class, Knuckles."

"Hell, I was just a kid," said Knuckles, then took a long swallow of beer before letting out a gigantic belch.

"There's something wrong here," said Mike, thinking aloud. "It doesn't play. She's the wrong type, it's the wrong neighborhood.... She's got to be government."

Knuckles gave him a startled look. "You think?"

"You got a better explanation?"

"What, FBI?"

Mike shook his head. "They're a little more subtle than that. The FBI always dress like college kids."

"DEA?"

"No. They dress like dirt bags."

"IRS?"

"That's a possibility," Mike replied, wondering as he said it whether all his deductions would hold up under an audit. But this was unwarranted paranoia. Any IRS agent in town would be after drug money; the IRS wouldn't have auditors in disguises waltzing in. "If she is a government type, we'll have to pass the word."

"Maybe it's nothing, Mike," said Knuckles.

"What do you mean, nothing?"

"Maybe she's just a tourist—a snowbird, you know?"

"In Alyce's Alley?" His tone sounded incredulous.

"It could happen."

With a look of disgust directed at Knuckles, Mike went back to watching the tourists. He knew that one day, if he just kept watching, the perfect tourist was going to happen by. Perfect was blond, built and easy to get along with, which, he figured, wasn't asking for too much. And when that happened, he was going to lure her into the Honkytonk, make her fall in love with him and then just possibly persuade her to move in with him.

In fact he was going to do everything but marry her. Mike didn't think of himself as the marrying kind.

THE FIRST THING Patty did was to check that the electricity had been turned on as she had requested. It was. Then she opened all the windows. She took note of the air conditioners—one in the larger of the two bedrooms and one in the living room—but ignored them. Her doctor had told her to avoid air-conditioning like the plague.

That led to the third thing: taking off her cape and her muffler, both protection against the air-conditioning in the plane, the airports and the taxi. Then she took off her sweater, her boots and her pants, and did a tour of the apartment in her Calvin Klein cotton briefs.

Except for the appliances in the kitchen, it was unfurnished. The closet space appeared to be adequate and the bathroom, although small, at least had a stall shower rather than a tub. She disliked standing up in tubs. The entire apartment had been painted pure white at her insistence, although the carpeting was in shades of beige. She detested beige. Still, it was neutral and she could always put in new carpeting if she stayed long enough to warrant it.

It was extremely sunny and bright because of all the windows and because it wasn't shaded by tall buildings as her apartment in Boston had been. She took out a pad and pen from her purse and added window coverings to her list of things she would need to get. These would be for privacy, not to keep the sun out. She loved a sunny apartment.

Patty noted the ceiling fans in every room. The doctor hadn't warned her against ceiling fans, so she went around and turned them all on. With the windows open and the fans on, the temperature became bearable. She wouldn't have thought, after spending the coldest winter on record in Boston, that she would ever again complain about heat, but she was bathed in sweat and feeling decidedly uncomfortable.

She unpacked the summer clothes that she had recently put away for the winter and hung them up in the closet in the larger bedroom, leaving only the smaller of her bags unpacked. She would take that one to the hotel with her that night. The movers would arrive tomorrow and she wasn't going to spend the night sleeping on the floor.

It wasn't the coldest winter on record that had precipitated her move, or even the seemingly endless snow that looked pretty drifting down and was one big pain to get around in. It was the way she had been feeling, which was finally diagnosed by her doctor as walking pneumonia. That and the news that the weather wasn't supposed to get any better.

"Go south for the winter," her doctor had told her, adding, "You can afford it. And I'll tell you, Patty, anyone who can afford to get out of here in the winter and chooses to stay is nothing but a masochist, in my opinion."

Patty didn't consider herself a masochist. As soon as she got home from the doctor's office she opened her atlas and looked for the southernmost point in the United States. She reasoned that whatever was farthest south was the warmest place to be. It turned out to be Key West.

The next day she called the Chamber of Commerce in Key West and requested the names of realtors who specialized in apartment rentals. She was told that it was the height of the season and she might have a problem finding one.

Not so. The first realtor she called told her she was in luck, that they had an unfurnished two bedroom available, which, she was assured, was charming. The six-month lease was in the mail to her in a matter of days. She signed it, enclosed a check, then, in the space of forty-eight hours, sublet her Boston apartment unfurnished and arranged with a moving company to take her furniture and household goods down. It was an expense, but she could afford it and she was crazy about her furniture.

She told only two people her plans: her mom, who thought it was a bad idea, and her best friend, Deirdre, who thought it was a stupid idea.

"You have no family down there," her mother said, as though Patty needed reminding. "You'll be all alone."

That was a plus, as far as Patty was concerned. Sometimes she felt smothered by her family; more than smothered, actually swallowed. "You're only a phone call away," Patty told her, realizing even as she said it that her family always reduced her to speaking in clichés.

"I hear there are lots of peculiar men down there." Her mother's voice sounded like the voice of doom.

"Are you referring to gays?" Patty asked.

"Whatever they're called these days."

"I'm not going down there to look for a man, Mother."

"You know I won't rest happy, Patricia, until I see you married with your own family."

"If you're referring to eternal rest, Mom, you've got a long way to go."

"You never know." That was the superstitious Irish coming to the fore.

It wasn't much better with Deirdre.

"I hear the men down there are all gay," Deirdre had said in a warning voice.

"I'm going down for my health, not to meet men."

"Yeah, but when you regain your health you'll want something to do."

"I'm just going to work and relax in the sun," said Patty, thinking that even seeing the sun would be great for a change.

"You'll be bored to death. Key West is a small town, Patty."

"I've been bored to death in Boston. Anyway, some warm weather and some peace and quiet appeal to me at the moment."

"I can't change your mind, huh?"

"No."

"Well, write me, will you? I'm going to miss seeing you. What'd Harry say about it?"

"I didn't tell him."

"You really going to dump him?"

"I already did, Deirdre—I told you that."

"So you said, but I didn't believe you. Harry's a hunk."

"But stupid."

"Would you care if I gave him a call? I wouldn't mind cheering Harry up."

"Be my guest." Patty knew even as she said it that Deirdre would be as quickly bored with Harry as she had become.

Her pneumonia didn't get any worse but all the talking on the telephone made her lose her voice temporarily.

When she had left Boston that morning the temperature with the wind chill factor was -20 degrees. When she arrived in Miami it was 81 degrees. Here in Key West it felt even warmer. She knew she had made the right decision. Not only was it wonderful to suddenly find summer in January, but Key West was much better than she had expected. And the apartment, which she wouldn't really call charming as the realtor had, could certainly be fixed up to look charming.

Right off she liked the looks of Key West. She had liked the drive from the airport, picture perfect with blue water, beaches and swaying palm trees. She liked the quaint wooden houses along the way, the lack of traffic, the people on bikes. And what she had seen on Duval Street, which appeared to be the downtown area, really was charming. She was glad her apartment was in the center of things so that she could walk places and not have to rely on taxis. And it made her feel at home; she was used to city life.

Not that Key West was a city, but she had been expecting a smaller island with fewer people. On the map it had been the merest dot. When she missed Boston, all she would have to do would be to look out the windows facing Duval Street and watch the people pass by.

Patty got into the only shorts she owned, which were running shorts, and slipped a T-shirt over her head. She would have to buy herself some sandals, but until then her sneakers would do.

She perused the list of things she needed and decided the grocery store would come first; that way the refrigerator would be stocked when she actually moved in and she wouldn't have to go out for all her meals. After that she would find out about telephone service.

The door to her apartment led out onto a long expanse of wooden decking, under which was the roof of the stores below. It was fenced on both sides and when she faced her apartment it looked like a New England saltbox painted pale yellow with white trim. At the far end of the roof was another apartment with two chairs sitting outside the door.

Looking over the fence running along the top of the inside wall of the building, she looked down into a long, narrow courtyard with shops surrounding it. She saw a sign saying Angelo's Pizza across from her, and above that what looked like an outdoor restaurant. There was a space behind the pizza place with picnic tables, and then a hamburger stand. Leaning over, she could see what looked like another restaurant at the rear of the courtyard with an orange cat sunning itself in front of it, but the other buildings were either empty or not visible from her vantage point. She knew her own apartment was directly over the Atari Game Arcade, which she thought was both coincidental and fitting. It was almost as though she had been destined to live in this apartment.

She was halfway across the roof and heading for the wooden stairs when the door to the rear apartment opened and a man came out. At first glance he looked like a Mexican bandit with his dark hair and eyes and downturned mustache, his body looking fit and muscular in his cutoff shorts, which was all he was wear-

He seemed to digest that information for a moment, then, "No kidding, so do I. I'm an artist." He stared at her as though waiting for her to challenge that remark.

Patty knew a street person when she saw one and if he was an artist she was the Queen of England. Nonetheless, she also realized that he was her closest neighbor—maybe her only neighbor—and if she got off to a bad start with him she could be in trouble. So she took his claim of artist with about a ton of salt and said, "I'd love to see your work sometime."

He visibly relaxed. "Listen, if there's anything you need, just give a holler."

"If you could tell me where the nearest grocery store is . . ."

"Fausto's is the closest," he told her, giving her directions to the store.

"Thanks. When I get moved in, come on by for a cup of tea sometime."

He looked nonplussed. "Tea? Nothing stronger?"

"I don't drink, if that's what you mean."

He gave a chuckle. "I'll give you a week. Everyone in Key West drinks. It's got something to do with living on an island."

She shook her head. "A good many people drink in Boston, too, but not me. It's bad for your health."

He was back to looking amused. "Well, thanks, Patty. I might take you up on the offer of tea one of these days."

She turned and headed for the stairs, aware that he was watching her all the way.

At the bottom of the stairs she paused to look around. At the rear of the alley was a place called Captain Harry's, and from down here it looked more like a bar than a restaurant. A Hawaiian shop took up all the space behind the Atari Game Arcade and had racks with colorfully printed shirts outside. On the other side, behind the hamburger place, were two small stores that weren't rented. Then there was Angelo's Pizza. Its entrance was on Duval but the alley side had a take-out window. Belatedly she noticed that three young men were looking out the take-out window, grinning at her.

She would have to remember to tell her mother and Deirdre that so far none of the men she had seen appeared to be gay. Not that she was really looking, of course. But then again, she couldn't help noticing, could she?

WHEN MIKE SAW NACHO come in the Honkytonk, he took a seat at the bar next to him. "Met your new neighbor?" he asked, still curious about the bundled-up woman.

Nacho grinned. "You referring to Patty McIntosh?"

"You've met her."

"I've not only met her, she's invited me by for tea."

Mike signaled to the bartender for a shot, then said, "I knew she was a kook. Mufflers in winter and now tea?"

"Mufflers?"

"She got out of the taxi all bundled up like it was snowing or something."

Nacho said, "Yeah, well, she'd just got off the plane from Boston. It's snowing like hell up there, you know. She was dressed pretty regular when I saw her. She's nice; a lady, if you know what I mean."

"They're all ladies."

"No, I mean it. She's different. Didn't flirt or nothing, you know?"

Mike laughed. "At least she has some sense."

"Hey, I'm not that bad. I know how to behave around a lady."

"You could've fooled me," said Mike.

"That's because you only see me in your place, and the Honkytonk doesn't exactly attract ladies."

Mike grinned, not terribly kindly. "Well, let me know how the Boston tea party goes. That's got to be a first for you."

Nacho winked at him. "Hey, man—I'm always open to new experiences."

Mike just shook his head, hoping that Patty McIntosh knew what she was getting into. If she really was a lady, then what the hell was she doing in this neighborhood? And befriending the Don Juan of the alley?

"She got a job down here?" he asked Nacho.

"Says she works at home."

Mike could think of one or two occupations done at home in their neighborhood and revised "lady" downward. It always surprised him how naive Nacho could be at times.

Then Knuckles was heard from. "Mike thinks she's government," he told Nacho.

Mike could see Nacho's muscles tense. But all he said was, "She didn't look government to me."

"That's the point," said Mike. "They're not supposed to look government."

"You think DEA?" he asked, naming the agency he had the most interest in.

"Could be," said Mike, wanting to watch him squirm.

"I think you're wrong," said Nacho. "I can smell DEA. I'll find out, though."

"How're you gonna do that?" asked Knuckles.

Nacho gave an evil grin. "I'm going to get real friendly with the lady, that's how."

Mike felt a momentary twinge of remorse for having voiced doubts about the woman, who, for all he knew, might not be anything more than an innocent snowbird. But then the twinge subsided as a blonde wearing shorts so short they defied description walked by and fantasyland took over.

PATTY HAD LOADED UP the shopping cart with groceries and could only stare in consternation when the checker said they didn't deliver.

"How am I supposed to get them home?" she asked.

"You don't have a car?"

Patty shook her head.

"You can always call a taxi."

With no other option, Patty called the local cab company. When the taxi pulled up in front of Alyce's Alley, she was left to unload the six bags of groceries herself.

She gathered the bags together on the sidewalk and then noticed Nacho sitting out on the porch of a bar next to Angelo's Pizza. Next to him were the two men who had been sitting there when she had first arrived. One was the huge man with the long ponytail who had helped her with her luggage and whose gigantic size had managed to intimidate her, even though she wasn't easily intimidated. Next to him sat the good-looking man with the great legs she had briefly noticed when she was trying to manage her luggage.

The last thing she wanted was to have that giant help her again, so she called to Nacho, "Would you mind watching these for me while I carry them up?"

Nacho was instantly off his bar stool and out on the sidewalk, then shouting over to Angelo's Pizza. Moments later each of the young men who had smiled at her earlier had a bag in his arms and was following Nacho, who was loaded down with two. She picked up the remaining bag and followed along.

When she tried to tip the young men after they had carried the bags in and set them on her kitchen counter, one of them said, "Don't worry about it; it was our pleasure. Come on down and have a pizza sometime. Just ask for Roberto."

And then they left, but Nacho didn't. He was looking around the empty apartment and finally said, "What're you planning on sleeping on?"

"My furniture should arrive tomorrow. I was planning on going to a hotel tonight."

"Hey, why throw away good money? I got an air mattress you can borrow for the night."

A hotel sounded far preferable to an air mattress and she was about to say so when Nacho said, "Anyway, unless you got a reservation, they'll all be filled. This is the season, you know."

"Are you sure?"

"Listen, didn't you get a load of all the snowbirds in town today?"

"Snowbirds?"

"Tourists, you know. They come down here to get away from the snow. The place is packed with 'em."

Actually, she would manage fine with an air mattress. All she wanted was a good night's sleep before the movers arrived anyway. "If you're sure it's no trouble."

Nacho grinned. "Don't worry about it. Frenchy was sleeping on it in my bathroom, but he moved out the other day."

Patty didn't even want to know who Frenchy was or why he had been sleeping in Nacho's bathroom.

"Thanks. I'll come over and get it as soon as I put the food away."

"No problem, I'll be right back with it."

She was just putting the last of the groceries away when he knocked on the door, then walked in carrying a rubber mattress the size of a double bed. "Where do you want it?"

Since the living room and the smaller bedroom were on the street side of the apartment and probably noisy, she directed him into the larger back bedroom. She was rather afraid he was going to find some excuse to stay, but instead he said, "Well, gotta get back to my drink."

"I really appreciate all your help."

He shrugged. "That's what neighbors are for. Want to come over to the Honkytonk for a drink? A Coke or something?"

"Thanks, but what I really would like is some dinner. Could you recommend a place?"

"The Honkytonk's got the best food in the neighborhood, too. Steak sandwiches, ribs, chicken. Unless you'd rather have pizza. Angelo's is pretty good for pizza."

"Maybe I'll be over later," she told him, thinking that a steak sandwich would be just the thing.

"See you later then, Patty," he said, going out the door.

When he had mentioned the air mattress Patty hadn't been thinking of things like sheets and a pillow, but it would be too rude to go to a hotel now after he had been so accommodating. Anyway, she wasn't all that spoiled, was she? She could remember spending many nights on the floors of friends' apartments when she was in college.

She remembered she hadn't been to the telephone company and saw that she still had time. The young men at Angelo's told her how to get there, and after filling out forms and giving them a security deposit, the people at Southern Bell promised her a phone in two days. And they were a lot more friendly than any phone company people she had ever done business with before.

In fact the whole town was friendly. Strangers smiled at her in the streets, cars slowed down and even stopped for bicycles and pedestrians, and she already felt at home in Alyce's Alley. And the whole place felt safe, unlike her neighborhood in Boston. And the weather! Imagine running around in shorts when everyone back in Boston was bundled up and freezing.

And best of all, she had finally managed to get away from the watchful eyes of her family. Not that she didn't love them, individually and en masse; it was just that they wouldn't allow her to lead her own life. And she knew it was because she was still single; if she were married, they'd breathe a collective sigh of relief and leave her be.

It just could be that she had stumbled across paradise. And if that was the case, she might never go back to Boston.

"WE'VE GOT A NEW NEIGHBOR," Nacho was telling Dirty. They were sitting upstairs at The Bull waiting for the pool table to be vacated and getting drunk in the process.

"More gay waiters?"

Nacho grinned. "Wrong. This one's female."

Dirty instantly looked interested. "A looker?"

"Not bad at all."

"You made any moves on her yet?"

Nacho managed to look relatively sober for a moment. "I don't think she's the type."

"Then what's she doing moving into the alley?"

"She's from Boston; I don't think she knew any better. Drinks tea, if you can believe that."

"I drink tea," said Dirty.

"Yeah, but that's all she drinks."

Dirty considered that for a moment. "Nobody drinks only tea."

"Yeah, I guess." Nacho checked out the pool table, saw that it was still controlled by the navy and ordered another rum and Coke. "The thing is, Dirty, I have a feeling she has bucks. And if we play our cards right..."

Dirty gave him an evil grin and ordered another beer. "You think she's the type good for a loan?"

Nacho gave him a disgusted look. "Can't you ever think big? The biggest thing you've ever done is pull that supermarket scam. And you weren't so successful at that."

"I've done some smuggling."

"Yeah, and what've you got to show for it?"

"Don't get on my case," said Dirty. "You think you're doing so well? You're getting free rent from Alyce just like me."

"But I'm also making some money on the side. Anyway, I think our new neighbor is worth investigating. She's no fed, I'm sure of it. I can smell fed a mile off. I tell you, Dirty, I think maybe this Patty McIntosh might just be our lucky break if we play it right."

"When did you ever play it right?"

But Nacho had noticed the empty pool table and didn't bother to answer.

Chapter Two

Patty didn't see Nacho as she stepped up on the porch and walked into the Honkytonk. That was fine with her; she felt like food, not conversation. Nor did she feel like losing her sense of anonymity on her first day of living in a small town. She had already answered enough of Nacho's questions. As it was, he knew more about her than her neighbors in Boston had learned in the past four years.

She supposed the Honkytonk could be described as rustic. If weathered wood, creaking ceiling fans and wooden chairs and tables with the paint coming off them was rustic, then it was rustic. In her opinion, it looked as though it was designed by the type of architect who worked with the radio on.

A long bar filled with tourist types whose pale faces indicated they were not avid beachgoers was to the left. In the middle were the tables and chairs. Three tables were occupied by people eating dinner, and in the corner were two young men with long blond hair and beards playing guitars and singing folk songs from the sixties. On the far right was a wooden staircase, which she assumed led to the rooftop restaurant she had viewed from her own roof.

Or terrace. Or deck. She really didn't know what to call the rooftop area that made up her backyard.

Patty saw the enormous man who had helped her with her luggage. He was seated at the end of the bar and she managed to avoid his eyes and seat herself at one of the tables with her back toward him. Which meant, conveniently, that she was also facing away from the singers. If she had spotted them before she came in she would have gone to a different restaurant.

The only restaurant with live music she had ever gone to in Boston was one Harry had taken her to where a chamber group had performed. She remembered the occasion well, as she had walked out on Harry between the soup and the main course. Harry, being Harry, had stayed on for the entire meal. Never let it be said that Harry ever let dissent interfere with his eating habits.

Thinking of Harry made her wonder whether Deirdre had called him. She hoped not, for Deirdre's sake. She had never really told Deirdre how boring Harry had been, mostly because she hadn't wanted to defend going out with him. Still, if you didn't listen to him and didn't mind going out with someone better looking than you, he was tolerable. Very early on she had learned to tune Harry out.

A menu was held out in front of her face and she took it, then looked up to see the enormous man's friend, the good-looking one she had seen seated on the porch earlier. He appeared to be scrutinizing her, so she lowered her eyes to the menu and pretended to be studying it. She had thought briefly of scrutinizing him right back, especially since he wasn't bad to look at. But she decided against it as good-looking men generally thought being scrutinized was their due, and she detested that kind of attitude. In fact she generally ended up detesting good-looking men, but that didn't stop her from being attracted to them. That was one of life's puzzles she hadn't yet bothered to figure out.

"Can I get you a drink?" she was asked, the voice slow, the speech soft.

"Iced tea, please."

"No iced tea."

"Lemonade?"

"Nope. But the margaritas are real special."

Patty looked up into eyes the color of green olives and this time he was the one to finally lower his gaze. "I'd like water, then," she said, "and a few minutes to look at the menu." That should have effectively dismissed him, but he still stood there.

"The conch steak is excellent tonight," he said, then appeared to be waiting for her to leap at his suggestion and order it.

Since she didn't have a clue what conch steak was, she ignored the suggestion.

Still he persisted with the tenacity of a salesman trying to close a deal. "If you don't care for fish, I might suggest the veal parmigiana."

Wanting to convey to him just how offensive his proprietary tone was becoming, she looked back up in time to catch the smile and the teasing look in his eyes. "I'd like a few minutes, if you don't mind," she reiterated, wishing he'd go wait on one of the other tables. In Boston it was a feat to hold a waiter's attention for ten seconds; here it seemed impossible to get rid of one.

The smile on his lips tightened slightly but he shrugged his shoulders in faint compliance and disappeared from her view.

She decided on the steak sandwich, which was what she'd had in mind anyway. Putting the menu aside, she waited for his return. When three more songs had been sung by the folk singers and he still hadn't come back to take her order, she looked around to find him deep in conversation at the end of the bar with a little man shaped like a kosher pickle. A kosher pickle dressed in baggy shorts and a hand-painted shirt.

She tried to get the waiter's attention to no avail, but while she was doing so a young woman in shorts and a T-shirt that said STAFF on it approached her table and said, "Have you decided yet?"

Patty gave her order and again requested a glass of water, and about ten minutes later both arrived. The arrival of her food coincided with the departure of the folk singers—and none too soon as far as she was concerned. She wasn't crazy about either electric guitars or folk songs and the thought that they might play there all night and, what's more, that she might be able to hear them from her apartment, had been disconcerting. She liked to choose her own music, not have it forced on her.

She had no complaint about the food, which was excellent. Just as she finished, though, the good-looking waiter who hadn't returned for her order came back to her table and, without even asking permission, took the chair across from her and casually stretched his slim legs out to the side.

She hadn't realized small towns were quite that informal or friendly.

"How was it?" he asked her, sounding as though he really wanted to know.

"It was fine." For some reason she found that her natural ebullience was in temporary abeyance, no doubt due in part to the fact that she wasn't used to having waiters join her.

"Good. We like our customers to be satisfied."

She gave him a chilling look. "If I could have my check, please..."

He folded his arms across his chest, right below a gold chain as thick as one of her fingers, and shook his head. "It's on the house."

"I don't see—"

"You're a new neighbor, right? We want you to come back again."

Despite the fact that the food was good, Patty had no intention of ever returning. This much informality was not to her liking. "I'd really prefer—"

"Wouldn't think of it. How about dessert? You tried the Key lime pie yet?"

"No thanks."

"You sure? We make the best in town." Then, with an easy grin, he said, "I'm Mike Enfield, by the way. And that big guy over there—the one who helped you with those suitcases of yours—is Bobby Knuckles, our bouncer."

She sat still, debating whether to offer her own name, and was just deciding against it when he said, "Glad you came by, Patty," and she briefly wondered where Nacho took his nosy lessons.

She gave him the smallest smile she could manage, wondering why such a good-looking man was paying so much attention to her. A little attention, maybe. But it was becoming excessive. As far as that went, shouldn't he be getting back to work?

Finally becoming unnerved by his smiling attention, she reached into her purse to leave a dollar for a tip, then said, "Thank you," and got up to leave.

She thought he would get up with her, but he continued sitting there. As she turned to go, he said, "Come back now, you hear?" But she didn't turn around, just walked out the door.

Good-looking really didn't adequately describe him, she realized as she headed down the street to buy some postcards. Sexy would be more appropriate: slanty green eyes in a triangular face with those high cheekbones and that full mouth that appeared to be perpetually pouting when he wasn't smiling. Anyway, good-looking just didn't cover it.

He had light brown hair combed straight back and long enough to hang over his shirt collar if he had been wearing a shirt with a collar. Instead, with his tight jeans, he was wearing a tank top that ended at his midriff, leaving an expanse of bare, suntanned skin. He had the kind of dangerous look about him that some rock stars had; what he certainly didn't look like was your average waiter.

But then she supposed she didn't look like your average mathematical genius, either.

Was he trying to come on to her? She thought so, but she wasn't positive. It was possible he was trying to make up for not taking her order. Or maybe he was that friendly with all the customers.

The question really was: If he was trying to come on to her, was she interested? It wasn't men she had come to Key West to avoid, it was the cold weather. Still, even if she had been looking for a man, it wouldn't have occurred to her to start checking out the men before she was even settled in. But at the moment, men weren't any dire necessity with her.

Also she had just recently ended a relationship and would rather like a breathing space before starting another. In fact, after breaking up with Harry she would probably need a good long breathing space. She remembered calling him—among other things—an opinionated pseudo-intellectual with psychotic overtones, then listening with relish to the sound of her apartment door slamming shut behind him.

She figured that even at this moment Harry was purposely leaving her alone and giving her a chance to cool down. She would love to see the expression on his face when he found out someone new was living in her apartment and that she was long gone. If Harry had any imagination at all, he would track her down, show up in Key West and sweep her off her feet. But that wasn't Harry's style. Harry would probably make the switch to Deirdre, figuring it was easier than putting himself out. That was more Harry's style.

Not that Harry really had any style. Harry only had looks. And even though it had been his looks that had first attracted her, after a while looks alone didn't suffice. That should tell her something, she supposed, only she wasn't in the mood for self-analysis.

Forget the waiter, she cautioned herself. So he was good-looking and sexy, so what? That combination usually went hand in hand with either egotistical and domineering or stupid and lacking in style. She would get settled in, get her health back, and then, when she was good and ready, she would see about a social life. Right now what she needed was rest and sunshine, not some island romance.

AFTER DOWNING his fourth shot of tequila of the day, Mike was sitting and contemplating the fact that a woman had just given him the brush-off. A woman who wasn't even his type.

Right away he'd known that. She wasn't blond and she wasn't curvy and that meant she had two strikes against her from the start. Plus, if she was government, she had struck out before she even got up to bat. Still, if she was government, it might pay to be friendly.

And, then again, it might be the worst possible thing to do. He was signaling for another shot when he heard some heavy breathing behind him and then Bobby Knuckles took the stool beside him.

"Slow night," said Knuckles.

"You ought to be glad of that."

"Hey, I like my job. And when it's this slow, I don't get to bounce anyone."

"Mondays are always slow."

"I saw you before, Mike, and I can't figure it out. I say to myself, What is Mike doing, going out of his way for that skinny broad? Mike never goes out of his way for skinny broads. She didn't look all that skinny before when she had all those clothes on."

"She's a new customer. I was just being polite."

"Plus she might be a fed."

"That, too."

"She's kinda cute."

Mike shrugged. "She's okay."

"The thing is, she looks like someone's kid sister. I hate it when a lady looks like someone's sister, you know what I mean?"

"You got any sisters, Knuckles?"

Bobby shook his head. "Do you?"

"No."

"So what'd you two talk about?"

"Not much."

Knuckles put a heavy hand on his shoulder. "Well, don't let it bother you none, Mike—she wasn't your type anyway."

Except now it was bothering him more because it was evident even to Knuckles that he had been given the brush-off.

Mike's first impression of Patty: no body, but he liked her face. Especially the eyes—the eyes had gotten to him. They were big and dark brown and showed absolutely no emotion at all. He hadn't liked her hair much. It was the same color as her eyes, cut with straight bangs that were so long they covered her eyebrows, the rest of it short and pushed back behind her ears. He didn't like haircuts like that on women. He liked long hair and the more of it the better.

The nose was small with some freckles across it and then across her cheeks. Real light skin, but then she hadn't been in the sun yet. Her mouth. Well, he hadn't exactly been crazy about her mouth. It didn't have the soft, kind of kissable look that he liked on a woman. It hadn't even smiled. Actually, if he had to describe her mouth, the word would be stubborn.

Not that any of that was pertinent to anything. She wasn't his type; he'd done his neighborly duty, and that was that. He could really live without women who were built like boys anyway. He'd leave it to Nacho to get friendly with her.

He just hoped she liked music.

Then two of the defense attorneys involved in the local Bubba Bust trial came in and the talk was about that day's testimony and about the cocaine that had been delivered to the deputy police chief in Chicken Unlimited boxes, which got a big laugh all around.

Along with the deputy police chief, two police detectives and a former city attorney, a local real estate woman and nine others had been indicted in a federal drug trial, and the locals were betting they'd all get off. Key West had always had a history of smuggling, and times hadn't changed much, even though the product had.

Mike avoided drugs himself, which made him something of an anomaly on the island. He figured that as a bar owner he owed it to the business to sample his own products and not someone else's. Anyway, he'd seen what drugs had done to too many of his friends. Key West was also Jimmy Buffett's "Margaritaville," wasn't it?

Yeah, give him a shot of tequila anytime.

ON THE BACK of a postcard with a picture of a beautiful sunset she wrote:

Dear Mom and Dad,

It's beautiful down here, a nice, peaceful small town. I feel better already just breathing warm, clean air, and I'm looking forward to getting a lot of work done. I'll write you a long letter in a few days.

Love,
Patty

On the back of a postcard with a picture of the Honkytonk she wrote:

Dear Deirdre,

Wrong, wrong, wrong!

This place is full of men, and so far they all seem straight. I've met more men in a few hours here than I meet in a month in Boston. Not that I'm interested, but I just thought I'd let you know.

Called Harry yet? Good luck if you do.

I'll write more soon.

Love,
Patty

SHE SHOULD HAVE OPTED for a hotel room.

First of all, there was the shower. Oh, it worked all right, lots of hot water, pretty good water pressure. It was the lack of towels. Patty finally made do with the roll of paper towels she had bought for the kitchen, but trying to dry her hair with paper towels wasn't wonderful.

Nor was the air mattress wonderful. It was firm enough; that wasn't the problem. It was more the lack of sheets. A rubber mattress against sweating skin just didn't feel very comfortable.

She remembered her terry-cloth robe and got it out of the closet, then realized she could have used it for a towel. Since she hadn't, she would use it for a sheet. She spread it on the mattress, turned off the ceiling light but left the fan on, then lay down on top of her robe.

Patty didn't know what time the movers would arrive but she hoped it would be early. Otherwise it was going to be a long day sitting around an empty apartment waiting for them.

She was just starting to list in her mind all the things she would have to do the next day when a voice that sounded right next to her said, "I'm afraid I'm going to have to take you in."

Patty stood up on the air mattress like Venus rising from her shell, clutching the robe around her. There was enough light coming through her window from the street for her to see she was all alone. But she knew she wasn't crazy. There had been a voice in the room.

"No, you don't have to do that."

Again she looked wildly around. Again she saw no one. As she stepped off the mattress she heard the sound of someone crying and she realized it was coming from outside her window.

She looked out and saw two policemen with a young man. A crying young man.

"Can't you just forget all about it?" the young man was saying between sobs.

One of the policemen turned to the other and said, "I don't think so. What do you think, Jerry?"

The other one put his hands to his head. One hand took off his cap and the other scratched his head. "Naw, I don't think so, either."

The clearly distraught young man started begging. "Please, couldn't you just throw it away? Forget you ever found it on me?"

"What do you think?" Jerry was asked again.

"I don't know. What do you think?"

Patty knew what she thought. She thought she was never going to get to sleep if they kept it up. She marched to the front door, turned on the outside light, then flung open the door in time to see three pairs of startled eyes turn in her direction.

"I don't know about you," said Patty, "but what I think is you're all trespassing and I want you out of here right now."

The cops looked at each other, looked back at her, then both turned to the young man who had now stopped crying. "Get out of here, kid," the nameless one said, "and don't let us catch you up here again."

Then they turned to her. Nameless said, "I didn't see a No Trespassing sign posted anywhere, ma'am."

"You mean I need a sign to keep people off my property?"

"It might be advisable," she was told. "The kids all come up here for privacy, if you know what I mean."

She knew all right; Boston wasn't behind the times in that respect. "And what do you come up here for?" she asked them.

"We try to keep 'em out of trouble."

"Well, I don't want the kids up here, or you."

Jerry took a stance with his fists on his hips and a truculent expression on his face while his partner looked at her with what almost amounted to astonishment. "Would you mind repeating that?" Jerry asked her.

Patty repeated it.

The nameless one stepped in front of his partner, who appeared to be trying to haul his civilized demeanor back in place. "Then I suggest you post some kind of a sign. They're used to coming up here and so are we."

"I'll post one tomorrow. In the meantime, I'd appreciate being able to get some sleep, which I can't get with you talking outside my window."

Jerry gave a short bark of laughter that was the opposite of contagious. "You think you're going to get any sleep in this neighborhood?"

"I'd like the chance to try," Patty told him.

As they said good-night, she closed the door and turned out the light, then watched through the window as they went down the stairs to the alley.

Not two minutes later she heard their voices again, but from a distance. She couldn't see them out of the back window, so she walked over to the side window that looked down on Charles Street. Sure enough, both a police car and a police van were parked down there and her two policemen were quoting her verbatim to several other cops, referring to her as "this broad." There was no way she could ask them to move away from under her window since it was a public street.

Ignoring her doctor's advice, she turned on the air conditioner, to a low temperature. Its noise effectively solved the problem of the talkative cops and even blocked out the faint music she had heard before.

But music she could sleep with. Conversations were quite another thing.

Right before she finally went to sleep, the face of that man—Mike—popped into her head. *Don't even think about him,* she warned herself. *Do not—repeat, do not—be taken in by another pretty face.*

Just remember Harry and be warned. Just remember what lay behind that particular face. People who traded on their looks were all losers, she was convinced of it.

Except that was about the last thing she wanted to remember. And with that thought she went right to sleep.

Chapter Three

Patty woke at her usual seven the next morning with sun streaming through the windows and her chest feeling about ninety percent better. Only one day in Key West and her health had already improved.

She spent a little time deflating the air mattress and folding it up, then drank some orange juice straight from the carton since she didn't have glasses as yet.

By eight-thirty she was bored with standing around, and getting hungry. She looked out the front window and saw that the street was quiet. The only business that appeared to be open was Shorty's Diner across the street. She liked to start the day with a good breakfast and decided she could watch for the moving van while she got something to eat.

The businesses in the alley weren't open yet, but when she got to where the alley led into Duval Street, she saw Nacho and another man standing there as though they were sentinels guarding the alley.

"Good morning, Nacho," she said. "I see you're an early riser, too."

Nacho turned bloodshot eyes toward her and even from a distance she could smell liquor on his breath. "Hey, Patty," he said, his words slurred, "meet Dirty, your other neighbor."

Patty looked up—way up—at the man looking down at her. He was on the borderline of a very tall man or a giant. He had straight dishwater-blond hair parted in the middle and hanging to his shoulders, a long mustache and a used face that looked as though it had been carved from rock and never smoothed out. But it wasn't his face that grabbed her attention. It was his body, or what was visible of his body, which was almost totally covered with tattoos. He didn't give the impression of anyone she would come to love as a brother.

Patty held out her hand to him. "Dirty?" she asked, sure she heard wrong, then revising this when she saw the word tattooed squarely in the center of his chest.

"As in 'dirty fighter,'" muttered Nacho.

"Shut up," said Dirty in a gravelly voice, then, seeing that Patty didn't know how to take his tone, said, "We're only kidding around. I love Nacho like a brother. An illegitimate brother," he added with a sly grin at Nacho, then ducked the punch Nacho was faking.

"Where exactly do you live, Dirty?" she asked him, not remembering having seen a third apartment in the alley.

He turned and pointed to the back, directly across the alley from Nacho's apartment. Now she could see, partially hidden by foliage, a small wooden room at the end. She had thought the outside stairs had led to an upstairs at Captain Harry's.

She turned to Nacho. "There were cops outside my window last night talking to some kid."

"They're always up there."

"Well, I told them they were trespassing."

Dirty gave her a look of approval. "You really told them that?"

She nodded. "I can't sleep if they're going to be talking outside my bedroom window all night."

"They're up there because of the kids. They go up there to smoke dope," said Nacho. "Sometimes we got more people on our roof than the Honkytonk has on theirs."

"What I was thinking," Patty said to Nacho, "was I could have a gate put at the bottom of our stairs with a No Trespassing sign on it. Would you mind?"

"I don't mind; I wish I'd thought of it. A friend of mine could make one for you cheap if you're interested."

"How soon could he do it?"

Nacho shrugged.

"I'll pay more if he can get it done today."

Nacho was nodding. "I'll call him. Listen, if he won't do it, I will."

"How's Shorty's for breakfast?" she asked, changing the subject.

"Tell Shorty you're a friend of mine," said Dirty, "and he might give you a discount. Depending on what kind of night he had."

"Thanks," she told him, again heading for the street. Behind her she could hear Dirty say to Nacho, "I give her one month here." If Nacho replied, she didn't hear it.

The diner had no tables or chairs, just one huge counter, and she took a seat where she could watch for the movers. She was sure they wouldn't come while she was watching—things never happened that way—so she was surprised when she saw the van pull up across the street just as she was finishing her cereal.

She asked for her bill and was taking out her money when she saw a policeman approach the van and signal it to move on. Only then did she notice that except for the taxi stand in front of Angelo's Pizza, the entire block was a no-parking zone.

She didn't stay for her change, just rushed outside and waited until there was a break in the traffic, then ran across the street.

She discovered her newfound friends out in force. Not only Nacho and Dirty but also the young employees from Angelo's—who must have just arrived to open up—were arguing with the policeman, but it wasn't until Dirty said, "Listen, give us just ten minutes, okay? We'll help out with the moving," that the policeman relented and told them to get a move on.

And then, without even being asked, her new neighbors, all five of them, began to help the movers unload the van and carry up her furniture.

It was for darn sure that would never have happened in Boston.

FROM THEIR VERY FIRST MEETING, the day and Mike hadn't gotten along. It had begun with the unbearable din set up by the leaves stirring on the tree outside his window, followed in quick succession by the sound of a car door slamming in the street, the faint voice of Nacho saying something unintelligible—and from then on it got worse.

Refusing to open his eyes, he discounted, but could not disperse, a growing apprehension that something was happening outside in the alley. Something noisy. Something he'd like to silence, only that would necessitate getting out of bed and it was too damn early to get out of bed. Generally speaking, he preferred to rise at the crack of noon, if not later. Sometimes a lot later.

Reaching across the double bed that had recently regained its single occupancy status, he grabbed his pack of cigarettes and a lighter, and miraculously managed to get one lit without coughing. Only then did he start his daily struggle to get his eyes open and won a close points decision.

Mike thought briefly of Cindi, who for a short time had shared his bed. She had fulfilled his three prerequisites, but despite that—or maybe because of it—it had been an obsession the way no serious thing could ever be. It had been a relief when she returned to Jacksonville.

But then it was always a relief when his relationships ended.

Now the noise began to break up into understandable parts. There were the remarks, such as, "Watch that end, lift it a little higher"; "Jeez, she's got enough furniture"; and, "Why don't one of you just watch the truck while we unload." Along with this were the occasional sounds of something heavy being knocked against wood. His erudite deduction was that his less-than-friendly new neighbor was moving in.

But at nine o'clock in the morning? As far as he was concerned, that was when most normal people went to bed. He didn't know why she was moving in at that hour, or whether it was by design, by chance or willy-nilly, but he would sure like the answer to that question.

Ms. Patty McIntosh was fast becoming a big pain in the luggage!

The thing was, what could he do about it? He stared at the wall, but failing to see any moving figures writing there and moving on, he decided the only thing he could do was voice his complaint. It wouldn't get him anywhere, but it might lower his blood pressure, which by this time was up in the low thousands.

In an actively bad mood now, he got up and pulled on a pair of cutoffs, then opened the door that led to the outside area of the Honkytonk overlooking the alley. And the pest's apartment.

With his eyes fixed on her door across the way where a mattress was being carried inside, he didn't see the puddle of water left by the clean-up crew. As he stepped into the water, his feet skidded and he landed on his rear end and went tobogganing across the floor for a rendezvous with the wooden railing. He must have let out a yell because the people in the alley all looked up as he entered the pattern for his final approach.

Applause greeted his landing and he looked down through the railing to see Nacho and Dirty looking up at him, along with two movers, three of the guys from Angelo's and Ms. Pain-in-the-kazoo herself.

"Hey, Mike, what're you doing up so early?" Dirty asked with an especially evil grin.

Wincing, Mike pulled himself to his feet and leaned over the railing. "What the hell is going on down there?" And then he really looked at the furniture being carried by the men. Red chairs, a red TV set, even red tables. The sunlight was bad enough on his eyes without all that red. What was she, some kind of nut on red?

"Patty's moving in," said one of the guys from Angelo's.

"No kidding." Sarcasm was his forte.

"You ought to see how good her place is looking, Mike," said Nacho, who looked halfway sober for a change. And Dirty was nodding in agreement. This from Nacho, who didn't know taste from tinsel, and

Dirty, whose own apartment looked as if it had been abandoned.

"She's even got a piano," was Dirty's contribution.

Mike gave up. The longer he stood there talking to them, the longer it was going to take her to move in, which meant the longer it would be before he could get back to sleep.

He finally looked at Patty, hoping at least to see remorse on her face. No such luck; if anything, she looked annoyed at his delaying tactics. "Try to keep the noise down, guys, okay?" he said to anyone who was listening, then turned around and went back to his pad.

If that Patty McIntosh had any endearing qualities, he sure hadn't discerned them yet.

THE MOVERS LEFT and Angelo's employees went back to work, but Dirty and Nacho stuck around and offered their help. They were both being so nice and polite and friendly she didn't want to refuse them, so she put them to work assembling her bed frame, something she didn't do too well, which resulted in its frequently collapsing.

She had the rest of the furniture arranged the way she wanted it and was unpacking her dishes when they finished and came into the kitchen.

"Even the dishes are red," said Dirty, sounding awed.

She grinned at him. "So are the sheets and towels. Red stripes, anyway."

Dirty walked over to the piano and started to play an incomprehensible tune with two fingers. "Where'd you find a red piano?"

"That was the one thing I couldn't find in red. I painted it."

Nacho lay back on her red wicker chaise longue and closed his eyes. "Why red?" he wanted to know.

Patty asked him if he'd ever been to Boston in the winter, and when he said no, she said, "Well, it's all gray. I just find red cheerful, that's all. I like some color." She had grown up in a house in shades of brown, her mother's revenge against all the dirt the kids tracked in.

"I love the red TV," said Dirty, followed by Nacho saying, "Dirty's a TV freak."

Dirty went over and hooked up her set, then said, "You have to have cable down here in order to get reception."

She turned to look at him. "Just for ordinary channels?"

"For anything."

She mentally added that to her list of things to do.

"I see you got two sets," said Dirty.

"No, I only have one."

"Then what's that thing in the other room?"

She saw that he was looking into her second bedroom. "That's my computer."

"What do you do with that?" asked Dirty.

"That's what I work at."

He nodded as though understanding, but she could see the perplexed look he threw at Nacho. But Nacho didn't catch it; he was now asleep and snoring.

"Listen," Dirty said, "if you don't need anything else, I'll get Nacho out of here. Once he's really asleep it's impossible to wake him up."

Nacho did come awake as Dirty was walking him out, though, and told her his friend would be by in a little while about the gate.

"Thanks for all your help," she told them. "Give me a couple of days and I'll have you both over to dinner."

Nacho and Dirty exchanged looks, then, in unison, said, "You mean a home-cooked meal?"

"I'm not a great cook. . . ." This was her own revenge against her mother's attempts to get her to learn to cook and thus snag herself a husband.

"Listen," said Dirty, "as long as it's not pizza, you got yourself a deal."

She was finding them a lot more interesting and friendly than her dull neighbors in Boston, except for that good-looking waiter who had complained from next door. And why a waiter was sleeping on the roof was something she couldn't figure out. She'd have to remember to ask Nacho about it.

MIKE WOKE TO THE SOUND of hammering and told himself it was only a dream. It couldn't be happening to him twice in one day. And then, very patiently, he waited for this particular dream to end.

It didn't.

Once again, with the definite air of a martyr, he put on his shorts and made his way—carefully this time—to the railing overlooking the alley.

He saw three things: Dirty sweeping up the alley, which was okay because that was Dirty's job; a tourist in a red, white and blue leisure suit who obviously considered himself one of the beautiful people; and lastly, Formica Freddie, who was hammering away on some boards for no obvious reason.

"Formica!" yelled Mike, his voice resounding through the alley so that even the tourist looked up at him.

"How're you doin', Mike?" Formica called back.

"What the hell do you think you're up to? People are trying to sleep, you moron!"

"I'm only doing my job, Mike, making a gate for the lady upstairs."

"Can't you do it somewhere else?"

Formica gave him an abused look. "How can I do that when it goes right here?"

Mike gave that some deep thought, or as deep as he could get at this hour, and couldn't come up with an answer. He hated to admit Formica was right, but after all, he was right.

Moments later he was back in bed with two pillows over his head, his heart pounding right along in rhythm with the hammer. Later, when the sound of a piano punctured his consciousness, he didn't even bother to get up. Without even a cat to put out, it would've been a wasted trip.

Someone was going to pay for this, he promised himself. Nobody was going to get away with messing with his sleep. And that someone was going to be Ms. Loony-tune herself.

PATTY WAS DELIGHTED with the way her apartment looked. The pictures were hung in the living room and all that room now needed was curtains and it would be perfect.

The kitchen was already perfect and she had more cupboard space than she had ever had before. The bathroom needed shelves, but Formica had told her he could put some in for her the next day and his charge really was reasonable compared with what the same work would have cost her in Boston.

The bedroom was also just right except for something over the windows. The second bedroom, which she now thought of as her office, held her computer table and chair and the computer itself, plus an extra bed for any friends who might decide to visit her. With the winter they were having in Boston, she was sure some of her friends would find their way down, which reminded her, she would have to buy some scenic postcards and send everyone her new address.

She had found out that the only department store in town was Sears, and when she had finished doing all she had to do, it was still only three o'clock so she took a taxi out to Searstown, thinking she might buy some furniture for her outdoor area. In that way she wouldn't have to go to the beach to do her sunbathing.

She ended up buying not only a chaise longue and matching chair and end table in redwood but also an umbrella table and four chairs. Her kitchen table only seated two, and this way, when Nacho and Dirty came over for dinner, they could eat outside.

On her way out of Sears she passed through the sporting goods section and stopped to take a look. There was a weight bench and also a rowing machine on sale, both of which appealed to her, but she didn't know where she would have room to put them. Still, she needed some form of exercise unless she joined a health club, as she had in Boston.

Then she saw the backboard with the net on it and decided she might as well enjoy whatever form of exercise she chose, and she had always been partial to basketball. She had never been tall enough to star at it, but she was proficient. She could pay Formica to hang it over her door tomorrow and the roof area was plenty large enough both for her outdoor furniture and some room in which to shoot baskets.

She thought it would be nice to get some potted shrubs and trees for the roof, but that could wait for another day. Anyway, the shopping center didn't have a nursery.

The way things were shaping up, it was going to turn out to be her dream apartment. She thanked whatever lucky stars were at work when she had been told of the place. She could just as easily have wound up with one of the boring-looking places she had passed on her way to Sears.

MIKE WAS SITTING out on the front porch of the Honkytonk being bombarded from all sides with rave reviews of the Patty McIntosh apartment decor. Even Formica, who had stopped off for one drink and was now on his fifth, was being heard from. It sounded almost as though the new neighbor now had a fan club.

"And you know what else, Mike?" Nacho was saying. "She's got bucks, you can tell."

"If she had bucks," said Mike, "she wouldn't be living in the alley."

"You wouldn't believe the low rent she's paying for that place," said Dirty. "I figure she'll be good for the occasional loan."

"You mean the kind you never pay back?" asked Knuckles.

"That's the best kind," said Dirty.

"I got some jewelry she might be interested in," said Nacho, warming to one of his favorite subjects, which was getting rid of hot items.

"I found a bike today she might like," said Dirty. "I'll get it painted red tomorrow and show it to her. She'll need a bike to get around on."

Mike gave a greatly exaggerated sigh. "Does this mean you're convinced she's not government?"

"No way, Mike," said Nacho. "She's got this computer; that's the kind of work she does."

"What kind of work?" asked Mike.

Nacho shrugged and looked at Dirty, who also shrugged.

"Didn't it occur to either of you idiots that her computer just might hook into a government computer?" Mike asked them, then watched as their faces fell.

"I don't know nothing about computers," admitted Dirty, and Nacho nodded in agreement.

Mike knew enough about computers to know that your average government agent didn't carry one around, but if she was on the up-and-up, she'd be better off if her neighbors retained their suspicions. What she didn't need was Nacho and Dirty conning her out of any money she might have. And if she wasn't on the up-and-up... "You guys ought to get her to show you what she does on that computer," he said to them.

"Dirty and I are invited to dinner," Nacho was bragging. "I guess we could ask her to show us then."

"So tell me one thing," Mike said to Dirty, who was at least being slightly more reticent than the others, "is the lady aware that you're both ex-cons?"

Dirty gave a shrug. "I never mentioned it. Did you mention it, Nacho?"

"It never came up in the conversation."

Mike nodded, having expected that answer. "I just hope she knows what she's getting into with you two."

"What're you talking about, Mike?" said Nacho, looking deceptively innocent. "Hey, man, we're her friends; we're going to look out for her. This alley isn't the greatest place for a lady to be living alone, you know."

Primarily because of the likes of them, Mike was about to say, then changed his mind. They were acting differently with her; he could see that. Nor had either of them made any derogatory remarks about her, as was their usual custom with females. Not that they both weren't crazy about women; it was just that they seldom respected them.

He must have stayed silent for too long because now they were back on their favorite topic of the day: Patty's apartment. He could only deduce that neither of them had ever seen a fully furnished apartment before. His own opinion was that any apartment furnished only in red had to be hard to take. Now blue . . . blue he could see.

Wanting to talk about something else—*anything* else—he said, "You guys seen the lead singer in the new group coming in tonight?"

Dirty grinned. "I take it from that she must be blond and built."

"Correct on both counts. Moreover, she's unattached."

"The singer back at Captain Harry's isn't bad," said Nacho.

Dirty leered. "You mean the one in the black leather?"

Nacho nodded.

"You guys have no class," said Mike.

"You go for blondes, I go for leather," said Nacho. "Anyway, I prefer hard rock to that watered-down kind you get."

"Not to live above," said Dirty, and they all laughed.

Knuckles spoke up for the first time. "I'd like to see that red apartment."

Oozing sarcasm, Mike said, "Well, Knuckles, why don't you go over and offer your help? Maybe you'll get invited to dinner, too."

"That reminds me, Knuckles," said Nacho. "You still looking for a place to stay?"

"Yeah."

"My bathroom's empty. Frenchy moved into his bus."

"Great," said Knuckles, smiling as though the offer had made his day.

At that point Mike tuned out the conversation. He couldn't concentrate, that was the problem. Lack of sleep would do it every time. And he had wanted to be in fine form to welcome his new singer that night.

PHYSICALLY EXHAUSTED by nine, Patty decided to make an early night of it. She showered, got into clean pajamas and was in bed by nine-twenty. The silence was as still as held breath and she was sure that no trespassers would disturb her sleep that night.

At nine-thirty Tuesday night, Patty found out the answer to two questions she hadn't previously thought of asking: why this particular apartment had been available, and why the rent had been so low. In a crash of sound that literally shook her walls and made her bed vibrate, a band started playing so loudly and so clearly that she felt she was sitting in on a session.

Except for the vibrations, she would swear that someone was standing right outside her window holding the largest ghetto blaster in creation turned up to full volume.

She got out of bed and looked out the windows but couldn't see any sign of trespassers on the roof. She put on her robe and slippers and went out the door to stand on the roof. Across from her, blazing with light and sound, was a band playing in the upstairs part of the Honkytonk, which she had thought was an outdoor restaurant.

Then she heard another band start up, this one from the direction of Captain Harry's, playing hard rock, while in the distance she could faintly hear a third band. She presumed this was from Sloppy Joe's across the street.

Still, it wasn't the other two bands that had almost thrown her out of bed, but the one only scant feet away. There were also loud screams and whistles coming from the multitude of customers flooding the upstairs of the Honkytonk.

She looked down into the alley and saw it filled with people, about a third of them heading for Captain

Harry's, about a third of them leaving Captain Harry's and the rest of them standing around and disturbing the peace. Her peace.

The music coming from the Honkytonk was so bad it was beyond belief. There was a lot of electronic equipment and a lot of bass and a lot of wailing from some singer who sounded as though she were dying. Patty only wished she would. She was sure it was some new kind of music devised solely to torture her senses.

Her peripheral vision picked up someone opening her gate, and she looked down and was about to yell at whoever it was when she recognized Nacho.

Tying her robe around her, she met him at the head of the stairs. "I don't believe this," she told him, waiting for him to agree.

"What's the matter, Patty?"

"This noise. They didn't do this last night."

"The Honkytonk doesn't have a band on Sundays and Mondays."

"You mean the rest of the time it does?"

Nacho grinned. "I can see you're like me. You prefer hard rock, right?"

"I don't like any music when I'm trying to sleep."

"You in bed this early?"

"I was tired. How late do they play?" she asked, afraid that he'd probably say midnight.

"It depends. They're supposed to stop at two, but sometimes they keep going if there's a good crowd."

"Two in the morning?"

"Hey, Patty, this is a tourist town. People come down here to boogie all night and the bars stay open till four."

It was déjà vu in reverse with a glimpse into her future. She tried to think, but it was like trying to do calculus on a runaway horse. In fact it was harder. Calculus on a runaway horse she could probably manage. "You mean," she said at last, "that there's nothing that can be done about the noise?"

"There's a new noise ordinance, but no one's enforcing it."

"Does that mean I could call the police and complain?"

He didn't look thrilled about that. "Sure. They'll take a decibel reading and if it's over the prescribed limit, they'll tell them to turn it down."

"Could I use your phone?"

He shook his head. "I don't have a phone, but there's one right down there in the alley."

"Are you going to hate me if I call the police on them?"

"Do what you want. Dirty's always calling them on Captain Harry's. The music doesn't bother me—I usually sleep days."

Nacho excused himself and went into his apartment and Patty took another look at the alley. It was predominantly men and she hated going down there, but she would go crazy if she didn't get any sleep that night.

She went inside and put on jeans and a shirt, then turned her outside light on and headed back outdoors. At the head of the stairs she looked down and felt herself suddenly caught and held in a blank concentration of eyes. There seemed to be young men everywhere, standing around like the statuary from an oversold cemetery, and all of them were staring at her.

She kept her eyes resolutely on her feet. Apart from other considerations, she wanted if possible to avoid falling headlong down the steps.

The telephone was being used by a man who had a Doberman with a homicidal appearance on a leash. She kept her distance, avoiding all the remarks she was getting from numerous young men and trying to make herself as invisible as possible. Only it wasn't possible. She didn't know where all the female tourists were, but they certainly weren't in Alyce's Alley.

When she got her turn at the phone she called the police station. The man who answered said, "Speak up, I can't hear you, lady," and she said, "That's the point, the music's too loud to hear anything."

She finally got her complaint across to him and he promised that an officer would be there soon to take a decibel reading from her apartment. She tried to tell him that he could hear the music just as well from the alley as from the apartment, but he said they had to follow the book on it and the book said her apartment.

She got back upstairs as quickly as possible, after pointing out to a couple of young men that sitting on her stairs was also trespassing. Then another man started up the stairs and, losing any cool she might previously have had, she screamed at him that he was trespassing.

He regarded her coolly. "No, I'm not. I'm going to see Nacho," he told her, and she watched as Nacho welcomed him into his apartment.

She decided to wait inside for the policeman and made herself a cup of tea to calm her nerves. Four cups of tea later the cop still hadn't appeared and she began to think he wasn't coming.

So she had two choices. She could go downstairs to the phone and brave the crowds once again or she could give up and live with it. Except there was no way she could live with it, so she went back down, told a couple of young men who proposed untenable suggestions to shut up, and called the police station once again.

When she told the desk sergeant no one had shown up to take a decibel reading, he said, "Officer Cruz said he couldn't go up there, lady, that he'd be trespassing."

It was obvious that he was either a complete imbecile or he had a very subtle sense of humor. "Please register my complaint for the second time and see that someone does something about this at once."

"Yes, ma'am," he barked into the phone, then the connection was broken.

When the officer arrived it was the nameless one from the night before.

"Nice gate you put up," he told her.

Patty thought he was being sarcastic and ignored the remark.

"I mean it. It'll make our job easier. Now we can just patrol the alley without worrying about up here."

He took a decibel reading, told her it was several degrees above the legal level of sound and said that he would go over to the Honkytonk and give them a citation.

"Does that mean they'll turn the sound down?"

"If they don't, they'll have to go to court and be fined."

"Thank you," she told him as he was leaving.

"I guess you got a thing for red, huh?"

"I find it cheerful."

"Yeah, well, it's sure different."

She closed the door and locked it, then sat down at the kitchen table and waited for the music to be lowered.

GARY CRUZ WAS STANDING in front of him with one of his "official business" expressions on his face. "I'm sorry about this, Mike, but we had a complaint."

"Come on, Gary—we're no louder than Sloppy Joe's and not half as loud as Captain Harry's."

"The only difference being you got a neighbor who doesn't like it."

"Who was it that complained?"

Cruz shrugged. "You know, someone in the neighborhood."

Mike recognized the calculated ambivalence of the answer and rejected any attempt at subtlety. "It was that loony-tune next door, wasn't it? Patty McIntosh."

"I wouldn't call her a loony-tune."

"What would you call someone who moves into the noisiest block of Duval Street and then complains about the noise? You know as well as I do, Gary, this isn't exactly a residential neighborhood."

"I know all that, Mike, but you also knew about the new noise ordinance. We haven't been doing anything about it, but we have to follow through on complaints. Come on, what's it going to hurt you to lower it a few decibels?"

"So Harry's can drown us out?"

"If it'll make you happy, I'll do a decibel level on them, too."

Mike let out a long sigh. "No, don't do that. It's not going to come to the point of complaining about each other. Okay, I'll get the band to turn it down. But if she thinks she's not going to hear it, she has another thing coming."

Damn complaining loony-tune!

Chapter Four

The singer's name was Sherri and she had long, tan legs coming out of her skimpy white shorts, and her low-cut blouse looked a breath away from slipping off entirely. She had enough blond hair to play Lady Godiva, but in Sherri's case it hung down her back. If her voice had all the tonal variety of a lead pencil, that was all right because the group drowned her out anyway. And without wanting to run the band down—and this would've been particularly difficult—they needed all the help they could get.

Best of all, she had her eye on Mike—a condition to which he was far from oblivious. Between sets she would sashay down from the bandstand and join him at his spot at the upstairs bar. She made climbing onto a bar stool an art. As her thigh would brush against his thigh, she would lean over far enough to afford him a view down her blouse clear to her navel, only it wasn't her navel he was interested in. Then, a small hand on his arm, she would breathe into his ear, "How about another rum and Coke, honey?'' and her wish was his command.

Which is what had just happened when Mike saw Knuckles giving him the nod, then glancing over to where Nacho was all but passed out on his bar stool. Mike seldom had Nacho bounced, but he frequently had Knuckles escort him home. Nacho had three drinking stages. During the first he was charming as only a con man can be. During the second he was all but comatose. It was the third stage Mike liked to avoid. That was when Nacho wanted to start a fight. And fighting, for Nacho, usually involved knives, at which he was proficient, even when drunk.

He gave Knuckles the sign to get Nacho out of there, then turned his attention to Sherri. ''What're you doing when you finish?'' he asked, pretty sure she'd be available. In fact, he was positive that this was what she was leading up to.

''Gee, I dunno. I'd kinda like to see the town, you know?''

He nodded. ''The thing is, when we close so does most of the town.''

''Like there's no after-hours places?''

''The airport bar stays open all night.''

''I like the sound of that,'' said Sherri. ''I can really get into watching planes take off.''

''The planes don't take off after nine,'' Mike told her.

She moved her head close to his so that he could feel her hair brush against his face. "We can pretend, can't we?"

"Sure," said Mike, thinking she was so easy it wasn't even much fun. Still, she wasn't bad to look at, it was just when she opened her mouth.

When she went back for the last set, he walked over to the railing and looked down into the alley. As usual, Harry's was drawing a better crowd than his place, but then Harry's got the navy and they weren't big spenders, so it evened out. He had half expected another visit from the police, but for some reason Patty's place was dark and she wasn't complaining tonight. Maybe she got smart and bought herself some earplugs.

Maybe she'd get really smart and move out.

AT THREE O'CLOCK Thursday morning Patty's biorhythms were way down. Conversely, the decibel level seemed to be way up. She could swear that the music from the Honkytonk was louder than the night before.

Despite having the air conditioner on high, the windows closed, two blankets pulled over her head and cotton in her ears, she could still feel the floor and the walls and even the bed vibrating from the beat of the music. But Patty was so tired she couldn't summon the strength to get up, get dressed and once more call the police.

It wasn't fair. Island paradises weren't supposed to have loud background music.

DIRTY WAS DOWN at The Bull having a drink, which was about the only bar he wasn't currently barred from, when Frenchy came in, his dirty feet trailing a path of mud behind him. Dirty personally didn't like Frenchy, but since he hung out in the alley a lot he tolerated him. Mostly what he didn't like about Frenchy was the way he hustled women. Not that Dirty didn't try the same thing, but Frenchy was more successful at it and that annoyed him. He didn't know how Frenchy did it; it certainly wasn't his looks.

All he could figure was that Frenchy always wrote songs about the various women before he hustled them. Dirty had tried writing poems, but so far all the poems had gotten him was a little sex, never any money. And money was what was in short supply.

Frenchy sat down next to him at the bar, saying, "How about buying me a beer?"

"I'm drinking on credit," Dirty told him.

Frenchy nodded a couple of times. "I'm dead broke. I need to make a score of some kind."

"Sell your bus" was Dirty's suggestion.

"Hey, man, you're talking about my home. But the cops are hassling me to keep it moving, and I don't have the money for gas."

"So find another woman," said Dirty.

"That's what I wanted to talk to you about. That new neighbor of yours, what's her name, Patty?"

"Leave her alone," Dirty warned him. He had plans for Patty himself, and he didn't want Frenchy beating him out.

"I hear she's loaded."

"No way," said Dirty. "If she was loaded, would she be living in the alley?"

"I wondered about that. Still, I figured that place would be easy enough to break into."

"Since when are you into burglary?"

Frenchy shrugged. "Since I'm getting desperate."

"She ain't got nothing to steal unless you can carry a piano out of there." He purposely didn't mention the computer; anyone could carry that and he figured it must be worth something. Getting rid of it might not be so easy, though.

"I gotta figure out a deal," said Frenchy. "I haven't been making a damn thing playing the guitar at sunset."

Dirty thought that was understandable. Frenchy must either have the biggest ego in the world or be tone deaf to think anyone wanted to listen to his singing. "If you figure out anything, and you need help, let me know. I could use some bucks."

"You sure about your neighbor?"

"Dead sure. Anyway, I like her."

"Since when did that ever stop you?"

Dirty thought about it, but couldn't come up with an answer.

SUNSET OVER THE OCEAN had been romantic, breakfast had been filling if not superb, and the walk back through town, hand in hand, with the streets empty, Key West at its picture postcard prettiest, had merely been meant as a prelude to what was inevitably to follow. Granted, there had been no stimulating conversation, but then that hadn't been what he was looking for. No, for what he wanted, Sherri would do just fine.

There was only one bad moment. The latest offshoot of the Bubba Bust trial was bumper stickers that had been printed up reading *This Car Was Bought With Drug$.* Someone, probably Nacho, had made the *C* into a *B* and plastered it on the front of the Honkytonk, so that it read *This Bar Was Bought*, etc. Mike didn't happen to see the humor in it and spent minutes pulling it off while Sherri stood impatiently at his side.

He escorted her into his apartment, drew the shades to simulate nighttime and help to conceal what a mess the place was in, lit one candle so he could see what he was doing and opened a bottle of champagne. Sherri was slipping out of her tiny clothes when he poured them each a glass, and just as he moved to offer a toast to themselves the sound of hammering shattered the moment.

For about two seconds he didn't believe it, then— "I'm going to kill someone," he vowed, putting down the champagne and charging out to the balcony. An unusual sight greeted him. Nacho was up and relatively sober, judging by the way he was hammering something to the wall over Patty's front door. If Nacho could balance on the top of a ladder, he had to be at least partially sober.

"What the hell you think you're doing, Nacho?" he shouted over the alley.

"Be done in a minute, Mike. Go back to bed," said Nacho, sounding like Mr. Sunshine. Nacho generally crashed in the alley at this hour.

Mike chose to believe him. If he hadn't, he would've been compelled to kill him.

"What's going on?" asked Sherri when he got back, and for some reason she was clothed once again.

"Nothing, forget it," Mike told her, thinking maybe they ought to dispense with the champagne and get right down to the basics.

He moved in on her and this time removed the minute articles of clothing himself, then pulled her back onto the bed. He stopped to listen for a moment, found that Nacho had been telling the truth and no more hammering was forthcoming, and moved Sherri over to the side while he began to pull off his shorts. He was relishing the sight of her when he heard the first *tap, tap, tap.* He froze.

"What's the matter?" asked Sherri with a distinct whine that was almost as annoying as the tapping noise.

"Shut up," he told her, trying to place the sound.

"Why're you telling me to shut up? You think you can just talk to me that way and it's okay or something? Like, who do you think you are?"

Tap, tap, tap-tap-tap—plunk!

"Did you hear that?" he asked her.

"I'm not deaf, you know." She started to say something else, but he clapped his hand over her mouth.

Tap, tap-tap-tap. He knew that sound from somewhere. Not from Key West, though. He wasn't familiar with that sound around here.

He pulled up his shorts and got out of bed, almost afraid to find out what it was, almost sure he was going to have to kill someone.

"Where you think you're going?" asked Sherri, sounding very much like a nag.

"Shut up a minute, will you?"

"And I thought you were some kind of gentleman."

Mike walked out the door and to the edge of the roof this time, the bright sunlight blinding him for a moment. When his eyes adjusted, he saw what he had never thought to see: Nacho moving fast. Nacho and Patty were playing one-on-one, the basketball hitting the backboard and creating a racket.

Looking down into the alley he saw Dirty, sweeping faster than he ever lifted beers, no doubt hoping to get into the game. He looked farther over the railing and saw Chris O'Neil, the cop on the beat during the day. "Hey, Chris," he yelled down to him.

Chris looked up, shading his eyes. "Yeah, Mike?"

"I want to make a complaint about the noise over there. It's disturbing my sleep."

Chris was shaking his head. "Can't do, Mike. It's eight o'clock in the morning."

"I know what time it is. I'm just getting to bed."

"Sorry, Mike, you can't complain about that kind of noise in the daytime."

Feeling totally frustrated, Mike turned around and went back into his room, just in time to see Sherri exiting down the stairs. "Hey, where're you going?" he yelled at her. Not that he really cared by that point, but he wasn't used to women walking out on him.

She ignored him.

"WHAT'S THE WAITER'S PROBLEM, anyway?" asked Patty.

Nacho caught the ball on the rebound and sunk a basket. "What waiter?"

"That guy over there was complaining about the noise."

"That's no waiter. Mike Enfield owns the Honky-tonk."

Patty was so surprised she missed her shot. "The owner? But he waited on me the other night."

"Sure, you were a new neighbor. He was just being polite."

So he wasn't an overfriendly waiter; he was an overfriendly owner. "I don't like him." That wasn't precisely the truth. She just didn't like his type. Or, more accurately, she didn't like being attracted to his type.

"Yeah, well, he doesn't like you much, either. He got a stiff fine as a result of your calling the cops about the music the other night."

"And it was louder than ever last night. I haven't had a good night's sleep since I moved in."

"You got to be a night person to live in this neighborhood, Patty."

"Well, I'm not a night person, I'm a day person. And I think I'm entitled to some quiet at night in order to sleep. If I weren't, there wouldn't be a noise ordinance."

She looked at her watch, saw it was eight-thirty, and was just telling Nacho that the game was over when Dirty came loping up the stairs, his long hair blowing out behind him.

"Hey, is the game over?" he asked.

Patty nodded. "I play from eight to eight-thirty."

"How about playing until nine?" asked Dirty.

"Sorry," she told him, "but I'm on a schedule. Get here at eight tomorrow and you can play."

Ignoring their looks of disappointment, she went into the apartment and showered, then fixed her breakfast. From nine to ten she would play the piano, then after that get to work on the software that was due in a few weeks.

As she ate she tried to concentrate on the physics program she was currently devising, but she found her concentration wasn't what it usually was. Instead, she found herself thinking about the owner of the Honkytonk and how sexy he had looked in just shorts, his hair tousled and his chest bare.

She was a little sorry to have learned he wasn't a waiter. She wasn't really a social snob, but she knew that his owning his own business made him more appealing to her than someone who earned his living waiting on tables. Not that waiters couldn't be perfectly nice people, but someone waiting on tables at his age would show a distinct lack of ambition.

And Patty admired ambition. She had never gotten into corporate ambition herself, but she liked making money. She liked spending the money even more. If she wanted to continue to be able to spend money, she had better get her mind off Mike Enfield and on to physics.

The only problem was he was physically interesting and physics was not.

After cleaning up her dishes and before sitting down at the piano, she opened all the windows and left the door to the roof open. Maybe Mr. Enfield would enjoy hearing some real music. She even found herself sadistically hoping that he'd like it about as much as she liked the music his band played. Which was kind of a surprise to her as she had never considered herself sadistic.

Perhaps a little Beethoven. She started the first triplet figures of his *Moonlight Sonata*, letting the melancholy notes drift out through the windows, but found it too somber for a beautiful morning in the tropics and began to toy with a couple of two-part inventions by Bach, whose mathematical precision and structure spoke to her.

She wondered briefly what people hearing classical music coming out of Alyce's Alley were thinking as she moved into Tchaikovsky. The unabashed Russian romantic. Never mind form and structure. Follow your feelings, your instincts, that's what he always said to her, and as she pounded out the first crashing chords of his second *Piano Concerto*, she let herself be swept away by the sheer force of emotion he packed into music. The melody, so beautiful, so perfect, opening the piece and then vanishing, never to be recalled again. Like every fleeting encounter with emotion—impermanent, vanishing. And also a big waste of time. Emotion, not the music.

She had run out of steam and was winding up her practice with a rather desultory rendition of chopsticks when she sensed that her solitude was being invaded.

"That's better as a duet," said the voice behind her, and without even looking around she knew it was her nemesis from the Honkytonk. She considered briefly the notion that her thinking about him had conjured him up. If so, she had better unconjure him or she wouldn't be in the right frame of mind to work.

"I prefer solos," she said, hoping the cool tone of her voice would be enough to discourage him. She continued her playing, ignoring him, but he wasn't so easily discouraged. Without waiting for an invitation, he sat down on the bench beside her and added a simple bass line.

He was sitting so close to her she could feel his body warmth, and she moved over a couple of inches. "My music disturbing your sleep?'' she asked sweetly, removing her hands from the keyboard.

''I think we need a truce.'' He was now improvising a simple countermelody on top of chopsticks and, in spite of herself, Patty was momentarily intrigued by the effortless way he turned a simplistic cliché into something interesting.

''Loved the Tchaikovsky, by the way,'' he said, and then, with an ease she wouldn't have believed, turned chopsticks into something Tchaikovsky could have composed.

Patty began to feel incensed that he played better than she did. ''If you know this kind of music, how can you stand to listen to that garbage you have over there at night?''

''I do believe you're a musical snob, Patty McIntosh.''

''I call it taste.''

He now launched into his own version of the second *Piano Concerto*, playing it with the passion it required and that she could never quite manage. She moved off the bench and stood looking down at his talented fingers, trying to suppress the awe she was feeling.

When he ended it, he swung round on the bench, leaned back against the keyboard and crossed his arms over his chest. ''We need to talk.''

''You're really good,'' she said, begrudgingly.

He grinned. ''In my misbegotten youth I had the idea of becoming a concert pianist.''

"What happened?"

"I got rid of my goals and have been enjoying myself ever since."

"Sitting around in a bar all night—"

"Do I tell you how to live your life?" Mike laughed at her, but in a friendly way.

Patty also crossed her arms and glared at him. "I'm sure that's what you're about to do. Never mind that you're already interfering in my life, preventing me from getting any sleep—"

"Preventing *you*? What the hell do you think you're doing to me?"

"I'm not doing anything to you." Patty found herself becoming defensive so he wouldn't know she was attracted.

"Playing basketball? Banging away on the piano? Did you really think I could sleep through that?"

"Those are normal daytime activities, Mr. Enfield. Furthermore, I would think if you own that place, you'd be able to afford an apartment somewhere."

"I have an apartment. Over the Honkytonk. Which was quite satisfactory until you moved in."

Patty moved across the room and sat down. "All right, you said you wanted a truce. What hours do you normally sleep?"

"Normally, from about six in the morning until about one."

"Very well. I normally sleep from eleven at night until seven in the morning. If you will have your band refrain from playing during those hours, I'll refrain from shooting baskets and playing the piano during your sleeping hours.''

He was looking amused. ''That's your idea of a truce?''

''Take it or leave it.''

''Lady, if I do that, it'll put me out of business!''

Patty shrugged.

''Look, can we be reasonable? First of all, even if my band didn't play, you'd still hear Captain Harry's and Sloppy Joe's, and they both play louder than mine.''

''Yours is the one I hear most clearly in my bedroom.''

He stood up. ''Sorry, but it's out of the question. I guess it's war, huh?''

''If that's the way you want it.'' War, she figured, would be a lot safer with him than peace.

He was looking around the room. ''What next? You got a trumpet hidden away somewhere? A set of drums?''

''Not at all. Next I go to work, and unlike your work, mine is done in silence.''

''On a computer, right?''

''That's right.''

He shook his head and started for the door. Just as he was stepping outside, he said, ''Well, at least I know one thing, you're not government. Government would try to be friendly.''

''What're you talking about?''

''Nothing. Just a thought.''

His attitude annoyed Patty no end, so she said, "You do understand, of course, that I'll call the police for a decibel reading again tonight."

"Do your worst, lady," she heard him say right before the door slammed shut.

The stupid part of it was that she really was attracted to him. He had an attitude that infuriated her, she hated him for disturbing her sleep, and she couldn't admire anyone who gave up his goals in order to waste away in a bar the rest of his life, but she was still attracted. Which meant it had to be his looks. Well, she'd always been attracted to looks and the men had always turned out to be idiots. At least with this one she knew he was an idiot from the start.

If she had his talent she'd be using it, just as she was using her talent for math. Not that owning a business was all that bad; it was the *kind* of business. What kind of an adult wanted to spend all his time in a bar listening to teenage music?

An idiot, that was who.

But a damn sexy one.

SINCE IT WAS A THURSDAY, the band came in for an afternoon practice session. While they were playing, Mike had Chris O'Neil take a decibel reading and had the band adjust to the legal limit. It was still loud enough to disturb Patty, but not loud enough to get him a fine.

He had been hoping the practice session would interfere with her work, but when it was finished and he was downstairs on the front porch having a drink, he saw her riding by on a red bike from the direction of the Pier House with a raft under one arm and a nose as red as the bike, and he deduced she had been to the beach. And if she had been to the Pier House beach, it showed she had bucks. They charged around four hundred a year down there just for the use of a few square yards of sand.

All of this meant she had class, a sharp mind and bucks. So what? Those were things he respected in a guy, but that he found totally unnecessary in a woman. Things like that would get in the way with a woman, make her independent, hard to get along with. Which summed up Ms. McIntosh perfectly.

"There's your friend," said Knuckles, sinking down in a chair like a dirigible making a landing.

"Getting real Key West with a bike and all," said Mike.

"Dirty sold it to her."

"One of his 'found' bikes?"

"Yeah. I think it was blue yesterday."

Dirty made a little money from just happening to "find" bikes, painting them another color, then selling them. Anyone leaving a bike in the alley was fair game.

"Maybe she'll be arrested for having a hot bike and that'll be the end of her," said Mike, knowing as he said it, it was wishful thinking. You just didn't get rid of problems that easily. He wasn't even sure he wanted to get rid of her that easily.

"Listen, if they went after hot bikes, they'd get half the town."

Mike nodded. He had a bike himself, but he made sure it was so rusty and disreputable looking that no one would even want to steal it. Just in case, though, he always locked it.

He grinned, thinking how tired she would be that night from all the sun she had gotten and how furious she would be when the cops told her his band wasn't playing too loud. Of course he was pretty tired himself. Maybe he'd take the night off on Saturday and check into a local hotel for some sleep. Or maybe he'd stick around and check in early Sunday morning with the singer in tow.

That sounded like a better proposition altogether. Sherri had no class, few bucks and if she had any mind at all she was able to disguise it. He tried to summon up the way she looked, but found instead he was seeing Patty's stubborn mouth.

Oh, well, he guessed he'd just settle for a good night's sleep.

A kid was going down the sidewalk selling the *Key West Citizen* and Mike bought a copy. The latest testimony at the trial was always good for a laugh. And right now he could use a laugh. For a change, though, the trial was nosed out of the headlines by something even more interesting. It appeared that the local treasure hunter, Mel Fisher, had hit the jackpot. His divers had come up with 13 gold bars, nearly 7 feet of gold chains, 414 silver coins, 5 silver plates and 16 emeralds set in gold.

What was even more exciting was that they had also found ballast stones and what might have been part of the *Atocha*'s mast, the *Atocha* being a Spanish treasure galleon that had sunk off Key West in 1622, and that Mel Fisher had spent the past sixteen years looking for.

"Take a look at this," he said to Knuckles, handing him the paper.

It took Knuckles awhile to read it, then he let out a low whistle. "Jeez, this is something else. These guys are gonna be rich."

"You talking about the treasure?" asked Nacho, appearing at the railing.

Knuckles nodded. "I bet a lot of the drug smugglers are going to be out looking for treasure now. It's just as profitable and you can't get busted for it."

Nacho was now reading over his shoulder. "Where's the profit if it took them sixteen years?"

A lot of people would be of that opinion, thought Mike, wondering for about the millionth time how he could love a place so much that was so corrupt.

Then he heard the conversation turn to Patty once again, and he decided he'd take corruption over that loony-tune any day. Not that she wasn't cute, if you liked the type, which he personally didn't. What's more, she was intelligent, which was something he rarely came across in Key West. It was mainly her attitude: She was abnormal. People moved to Key West because it was wide open, a real party town, and what did Ms. McIntosh do? Move in and try to live by Boston rules. The kind of rules he'd been glad to leave behind. Things like the work ethic and schedules and sleeping nights.

All of which meant they had nothing in common, so why the hell was he becoming obsessed with her?

Well, if it was war she wanted, it was war she'd get. He had a few secret maneuvers up his sleeve, one of which was to have the band play seven nights a week. No sense in letting her catch up on her sleep.

As for his sleep, he figured he could do without it longer than she could. He'd give her a week, then he'd bet she'd be on her merry way back to Boston.

DIRTY DIDN'T READ newspapers, but he always watched the news on television. When the newscaster from Miami mentioned Key West, Dirty half sat up on his bed. When treasure was mentioned, he sat all the way up and listened closely.

When gold and emeralds were mentioned, and also the fact they were right now on their way to Key West, a light went on in his head and visions of easy money began dancing before his eyes.

It would all depend on whether Nacho thought he could fence the stuff. But hell, Nacho could fence anything.

Chapter Five

Dear Deirdre,

I was wrong, paradise this is not.

First of all, I think I got taken on this apartment. At first I thought the setting was quaint and charming, my apartment being in a place called Alyce's Alley. Forget quaint and charming. I am surrounded by bars with live bands playing the worst kind of rock and it's driving me up the wall.

You know me, I'm a morning person. Well, the bands don't quit until about four in the morning and the noise is as clear as if I were wearing a Walkman on my head with the sound turned up high. I'm not exaggerating, either.

My "straight" neighbors are straight all right, but the biggest con artists I've ever met. The one who lives in the apartment behind me, Nacho, calls himself an "artist" but has a steady stream of clients going up to his apartment. And he isn't dealing in art. He also rents out his bathroom, currently to the most enormous man I've ever seen.

My other neighbor, Dirty, has no visible means of support and I haven't figured out his game yet. Both of them are friendly and nice to me and I can tell they think I'm Miss Gullible, and I'll go on letting them think that and keep my eyes open at the same time.

Here's the interesting part. The guy who owns the Honkytonk next door, which has the band that really drives me up the wall, is the most gorgeous man I've met in ages. At the moment we have a feud going over the noise. His band keeps me awake nights, so now I'm keeping him awake days. How he can stand his band I don't know because he plays the piano beautifully.

Don't worry, though, I'm only having fun. Nothing serious, I just like his looks. As usual.

I'll keep you posted on the war. Meanwhile, I want to get some sleep tonight.

Did you ever call Harry?

Love,
Patty

ON THURSDAY NIGHT Patty called the police on the Honkytonk. The same two officers arrived at her door, took a decibel reading, and informed her that the band at the Honkytonk was under the legal sound level.

Tired and furious, Patty shouted at them—which was the only way to be heard over the noise of the band—"Can't you hear them yourselves?"

"Sure, but it's still legal, ma'am. This is the downtown area, you know, not a residential neighborhood."

"Well, this is a residence," countered Patty.

"Sorry, lady, you're going to have to live with it."

When they left, Patty got back in bed. That she was fuming was an understatement. Have to live with it? Like hell she had to live with it.

She had a talent for devising computer strategy games. If she could solve the kind of problems those games presented, she certainly could solve the problem of the music next door.

Mike Enfield wanted war? She'd give him war!

WHEN THE TWO MEN arrived at her door Friday morning, she was ready for them.

"We were told this was an emergency," one of them said. "We were told we'd be paid extra."

"That's right," said Patty. "There's only one condition. If anyone—anyone at all in the alley—asks you what you're doing up here, you're installing insulation in the attic to cut down on the cost of the air-conditioning. You understand?"

They exchanged looks, then shrugged. "Sure, lady, whatever you say," said the self-appointed spokesman.

"As long as you do that, there'll be an extra hundred in it for both of you."

"What're we installing, J.J.?" asked the spokesman.

"Insulation," said his partner.

"That's what I figured."

Leaving them to their work, Patty went to the Pier House beach for the day. She basked in the sun all morning, reading a book; she had a lovely conch salad for lunch at the raw bar; and in the afternoon she moved to the shade of one of the palm trees and took an extended nap. Before going home, she moved from the beach up to the pool and swam a few laps since she hadn't got in her exercise for the day.

At five o'clock she returned home. The men were just finishing. Before she paid them, she turned on her stereo in the living room full blast, then shut herself in the bedroom. It was beautiful. Better than beautiful, it was glorious.

In her newly soundproofed room she couldn't hear a thing.

As soon as the men left, she gave a shout of joy. She had not only won the battle, she had won the war.

The labor and materials had cost her over a thousand dollars and someone was going to pay for that. Not in money, but there were other, more pleasurable ways.

The one who was going to pay was Mike Enfield. And revenge was going to be sweet.

FRIDAY NIGHT Patty slept in silence, proving to her that money could indeed buy happiness.

Since she didn't work on weekends, on Saturday morning she played an extended game of basketball with Dirty, followed by a rousing session at the piano. After that she decided to sunbathe on the roof rather than go to the beach. She brought out her stereo, a glass of iced tea and a book, then settled herself on the chaise.

What she didn't play on the stereo was classical music. Because of Mike's background, she didn't think classical music would be jarring enough and she wanted to make sure that the music she played indeed jarred him out of his sleep.

She had brought back a cassette from her trip to Greece, and if there was any music in the world more jarring than Greek music, she hadn't heard it. To say it was atonal was to compliment it.

She put in the cassette, turned the volume up all the way, then waited for the first blasting sounds of the bouzoukis. With the speakers pointed toward the Honkytonk and earplugs in her ears, she found she could tolerate it.

With a satisfied smile, she settled back and waited.

MIKE HAD NOTED the extended length of the basketball game. He had also noted the fact that Patty McIntosh spent her afternoons at the beach. So when the first strains of the music were heard, he didn't immediately connect it to her. In fact he didn't even connect it to music. It sounded more like a burglar alarm going off, and he patiently waited it out. Burglar alarms going off were a regular occurrence, but eventually they were stilled.

When enough time had elapsed to cut off numerous burglar alarms and the screeching continued, he patiently got out of bed and headed outside. He still wasn't connecting it to Patty, but it did sound as though it was coming from the alley.

He saw the speakers first. All four of them, and all of them pointing in his direction. He could also see the top of a head on the chaise longue. It could be Nacho passed out, of course, but he had a feeling it wasn't.

Well, he had several choices. He could complain, but he knew it wouldn't do any good. Plus, he didn't want to give her the satisfaction. He could shoot the speakers to pieces, only he didn't have a rifle. And even if he had, he didn't want to end up in jail.

He could also drink enough tequila so that he'd pass out and no longer hear the music. That was the best solution he could come up with. He got a little satisfaction out of knowing that she couldn't be enjoying that god-awful sounds any more than he was.

The hell with the fine. Tonight the decibel level was going to go up high enough to blow her through the roof!

PATTY DIDN'T TURN DOWN the music until around three, when Nacho staggered out of his apartment, and from the looks of his hangover she figured the noise might kill him.

"Hey, Patty," he said, sitting down at her umbrella table. "What do you say we have a barbecue tonight?"

"You mean out here?"

"Yeah. I could cook up a bunch of chicken and get a keg of beer. You could meet some of the people around here, get acquainted. They're all curious about you."

Patty couldn't think of any good reason why not. She would be able to sleep with her soundproofing, but the music would drown out the TV set in the living room and she had nothing else to do. "Okay with me," she said. "I'll make a salad."

"How about we split the cost? You pay for the chicken and I'll provide the beer and do the cooking. I'll even go to the grocery store."

"Sure, how much do you want?"

"I dunno; maybe forty?"

Patty went inside and got forty dollars, then told him what she'd need for the salad. "And get some paper plates and napkins, too."

"Great," he said, getting up and stuffing the money in his pocket. "I'll spread the word. We'll start about eight, okay?"

What was going to be great about the party, thought Patty, was that even though it was going to be right outside her window, and even though it might go on late, she'd be able to go home and get to sleep anytime she wanted. She wouldn't be able to hear a thing.

MIKE AND FRENCHY were leaning on the railing looking across the alley. "What's happening over there?" he asked Frenchy.

"Nacho's giving a party. Free food and booze. I'm going over there myself."

"Their music's as loud as the band's."

Frenchy nodded. "Yeah, that neighbor of his has a quadraphonic sound system. I hear she's got bucks."

"Leave her alone, Frenchy," he said, wondering why he was suddenly coming to Patty's defense.

"Hey, man, it's open season on snowbirds."

"She's not a snowbird, she's a neighbor."

"Come on, Mike, give me a break. You know what I got out of the last one?"

"Yeah. A boat."

"No, that was the one before. A bus, man—you ought to see it. I got it all fixed up like one of those mobile homes. Yeah, I think I'll go over there now, play a little guitar music for her..."

"How does it feel being a gigolo, Frenchy?"

Frenchy grinned, showing his yellow teeth. "It feels well fed, Mike; yeah, that's exactly how it feels."

Frenchy left and Mike stayed on, watching the display of lightning in the west. And if there was enough of that lightning, there would be a blackout for sure. A common occurrence in the Keys, where even a windstorm invariably knocked out cable TV.

He saw Nacho looking over at him and waving. "Come on over," Nacho yelled to him, but Mike just shook his head. In the good old days, the days before Patty McIntosh, he probably would have taken a break and checked out the party.

He was just turning around to go back to the bar when the lights went out. Instant silence filled the alley. All the bands were out of action, and also Patty's quadraphonic system. He hurried to the bar, saw that the waitresses were already putting candles out on the tables, then went up on the bandstand and announced to the customers that they should hang in there, the lights would be on soon and the band would make up for the lost time by playing later than usual.

He went back to the railing to see how the party was faring. Candles were appearing over there, too, and he could hear Frenchy taking advantage of the absence of music, playing his guitar and singing the only folk song Mike had ever heard him sing, probably the only one he knew. Then others began to join in, and pretty soon he saw his customers crowding up beside him, looking across the alley to where the only action was, and then, like moths drawn to a light, they started going down the stairs and heading for the free party.

In five minutes flat there were more people on Nacho's roof than there were on his. If you can't fight 'em, he figured... He went down to the alley to join them.

"Hey, Mike," said Nacho, "help yourself to some chicken. Patty made some salad, too—it's over there on the table."

"No thanks," said Mike, although the barbecue sauce smelled damn good. A quick glance around the roof showed him every lowlife in town—except his customers, of course, who were mostly tourists.

He saw Dulcie, the youngest hooker in the alley, sitting next to Patty and talking a mile a minute, which was something he had to hear. Dulcie could use more four-letter words in one sentence than anyone he knew, and he wanted to see how the lady from Boston was reacting.

To his surprise, the conversation was about computer games, and Dulcie, for once, was watching her language.

Hell, maybe he was wrong. Maybe what the alley needed was a good influence.

Yeah, just like it needed a blackout on the busiest night of the week.

PATTY, SECURE in the knowledge that she had won the war, gave Mike a smile when she saw him approaching. She saw him hesitate, then look around to see whom she was smiling at. Well, he ought to be suspicious; he didn't know the half of it.

She liked the way he walked, kind of rolling from the hips the way baseball players walked. Only in a baseball uniform it looked like a swagger; in shorts it was just plain sexy. She kept smiling until he realized the smile was meant for him. Then, when he was close enough, she said, "Thanks. That was kind of you to shut off the music for me."

Now he was smiling, but it wasn't the kind of smile that held humor. "You're welcome. I thought it was the least I could do when you so kindly provided me with soothing background music to my sleep today."

Patty had to bite her lip to keep from laughing out loud. "I had a feeling you might be a devotee of the bouzouki. It has the same kind of quality that band of yours possesses."

Even by candlelight, she could see the sudden gleam in his eyes. "I wouldn't be surprised if tomorrow you will cross the Aegean and treat me to some lovely Turkish music."

Patty couldn't hold back the laughter at that. If there was one thing in the world worse than Greek music, it was Turkish, whose singers all sounded as though they were dying an agonizing death, no doubt at the hands of the Greeks. "No, not tomorrow. Sunday is a day of rest and I'm going to learn how to snorkel."

"Snorkel?"

"Yes. I always wanted to learn and I hear it's great around here."

"It's fantastic. I'll take you snorkeling."

Instant suspicion. "I appreciate the offer, Mr. Enfield, but I can't help thinking that my drowning would come as a boon to you."

He smiled, and it looked genuine this time. "And mine to you, don't forget."

"All right, Mike, we'll call a truce for tomorrow. What time do we leave?"

"Would you let me sleep till noon?"

"You mean without benefit of basketball practice?"

"That's exactly what I mean."

"Certainly. Snorkeling will be enough exercise."

Dulcie had moved on by now, and Mike took her seat next to Patty. "Tell me something, Patty. Why the interest in basketball?"

"My earliest ambition was to play with the Celtics."

"What happened?"

"I stopped growing."

"Why don't you get that basketball of yours and we'll shoot a few?"

"You play basketball?"

"Not since I was a kid, and then not very well."

He was being a shade too cagey to inspire confidence. He had probably been the star of his school's team and was trying to con her. In fact he was being altogether too friendly and she wondered what he was up to. "No thanks, maybe some other time. I think I'm going to take advantage of the absence of music and get some sleep."

"Look, Patty, you got to realize there's a difference here. I've always had bands over there; it wasn't something I dragged out just to annoy you."

"Meaning my music is."

"Well, isn't it?"

She was forced into either lying her head off or conceding his point. Honesty won out, but it was a close decision. "All right, the Greek music, yes. But I always exercise and practice the piano in the morning."

"You fight dirty, don't you?"

"War is hell, Mike."

He stood up. "I guess I'll get back to work. When I see you in the morning I'll be waving a white flag."

TWENTY MINUTES LATER, when the power was restored, Mike was still wondering why he had offered to take her snorkeling. Not that he didn't like snorkeling, he did it every chance he got. It just wasn't something he preferred doing with novices, and female novices at that. Women had their place in his life, but that place usually wasn't out on his boat.

Maybe that was it. Maybe it was because he didn't think of her as a woman, just as a loony-tune nuisance who was obviously his equal when it came to being stubborn.

Not that it might not be a bad idea to start treating her like a woman. Maybe a little sweet talk would soften her up, get her to ease up on the volume of noise she was putting out every morning. But somehow he doubted it. He had the crazy idea that this was one woman on whom sweet talk would not have the desired effect.

Well, nothing ventured, etc., and the invitation had at least ensured him a peaceful Sunday morning sleep. The idea pleased him so much he made it a point to ignore Sherri the rest of the night. Which wasn't all that difficult to do. He was beginning to think she was just one step up from Dulcie, and not a giant step at that.

PATTY COULD FEEL a slight vibration in the room when the music resumed, but that was all. The rest was blissful silence.

The party had been nice, as had all the people she had met. Even the folk singers that sang downstairs in the Honkytonk in the early evening were there, and when they weren't singing she found she liked them.

Nacho appeared to know everyone in town. There had been several lawyers and a judge and even a couple of politicians there. There had been some businessmen down from Miami for the fishing, or so they said. They had more gold chains around their necks than she had ever seen, which made her question just what business they were in. And the young girl, Dulcie, had been sweet, although what a fifteen-year-old was doing in the alley at that hour she didn't know. Well, that wasn't quite true, she had a suspicion. She just didn't want to believe it.

Mike had been a surprise. Not only by being friendly, but in saying he'd take her snorkeling. She had a feeling he was up to something. Maybe he felt if he took her snorkeling she'd be in his debt and she'd knock off the harassment. If so, he didn't know the first thing about her.

On the other hand, she did feel a twinge of guilt about the Greek music. He had been right when he pointed out that his band had always played, that it wasn't personally directed at her. Still, someone was going to pay because she had been forced to expend a large sum of money just to get the same amount of sleep that everyone was entitled to.

Maybe the realtor who had rented her the apartment was more at fault than Mike. She could probably break the lease, citing as the reason that she hadn't been told of the noise. The thing was, she didn't want to move. She liked the apartment and she liked the neighborhood. And now that she had the soundproofing, she could live with the music.

But the basketball was staying. She might consider closing the windows when she practiced her piano, but she still needed to get her exercise.

She wasn't ending the war just because some good-looking man asked her to go snorkeling. That wasn't it at all. It was just that she suddenly realized that she was the one provoking it, and since she had solved her own problem, it hardly seemed fair to keep punishing him, although she had to admit she had been starting to get into it. Lately, she had actually been enjoying it.

Well, she'd always known she wasn't a pacifist.

AFTER THE PARTY Dirty told Frenchy to stick around, then cornered Nacho and said, "We need to talk in your apartment."

"What's up?" asked Nacho, none too sober.

"I got this great idea."

Nacho had heard Dirty's great ideas before, but what the hell, it was too early to go to bed.

So the three of them sat around Nacho's living room sharing a bottle, and when he was sufficiently mellow, Dirty said, "You guys read about the treasure coming into town?"

"Hell, yes, who hasn't," said Frenchy.

"I heard about it at the Honkytonk," said Nacho, who only read when he was in jail and there was nothing else to do.

"I say we steal it," said Dirty.

"Hit the museum?" asked Frenchy.

Dirty nodded, looking smug and superior.

"I don't do burglaries," said Nacho, sounding as smug and superior as Dirty was looking.

"You'll be the fence," said Dirty.

They all sat there thinking about it for a moment, then Frenchy said, "It could be done. I can't understand why nobody thought of hitting the museum before. That place has got to have millions in gold."

"Just waiting to be taken," added Dirty.

"Beautiful," said Nacho. "I got a connection who'll melt the gold down for us and we can sell it by the ounce."

"By the pound," said Dirty, then he started chuckling. "Our ship is really coming in."

"What we gotta do," said Frenchy, "is check the place out. I've never even been to that museum."

Dirty gave a grin of evil proportions. "You haven't heard the best part. I got the idea tonight. The place is bound to have security, but I figure we'll hit it in the next blackout when any burglar alarms they have won't be working."

Frenchy said, "Yeah, but how do we know when that'll be?"

"What I figure," said Dirty, "is you should stay close to the alley so when it happens we can run over there. What's it, about two minutes from here?"

"Next good rain'll do it," predicted Nacho.

"So, it's on?" asked Dirty.

"I'm in," said Frenchy.

"I want a third for fencing," said Nacho.

They sealed their partnership with a toast from a bottle of tequila Dirty had swiped from The Bull.

Chapter Six

They biked over to the marina where Mike kept his boat docked. It was a small motorboat with room enough for four, and when Mike stopped to fill it up with gas, they got some soft drinks and sandwiches to take with them. He already had the snorkeling gear on board.

What was disconcerting to Patty was that she was feeling so at ease with him. She barely knew the man, they had this feud going, and yet neither seemed compelled to make nervous conversation and the talk they had seemed natural, as did the silences. She would've figured it was because there were no sexual undertones to it, except that wasn't precisely the case. She was definitely attracted, although she couldn't tell about him one way or the other. He just seemed to be out for a pleasant day and that was fine with her.

The island was only one mile by three, so he took her on a tour around it first. He showed her all the land the navy owned and she recognized the Pier House when they passed it. It was strange, but out on the water Key West looked small and defenseless and she said so to Mike.

"Wait till hurricane season," he told her.

"Are there always hurricanes?"

"There's always the threat. Don't worry, though, for a big one they'll evacuate everyone by air."

Patty thought that sounded exciting. The worst she'd ever suffered from the weather was being snowed in on a couple of occasions.

There was an island across from the Pier House that he told her was Christmas Tree Island, and he motored over so that she could look at it. He put down the anchor and they waded in, seeing evidence of people camping out there. They shortly returned to the boat, however, when swarms of mosquitoes started attacking.

"You know," he said, "you could live on that island for nothing."

"Why would I want to live there?"

He shrugged. "I just thought it might appeal to you. No live bands, no noise at all—you'd sleep like a baby."

"No electricity, no water."

"You don't like roughing it?"

She shook her head, wondering if maybe he had been slightly tempted to leave her there and take off. He probably would have if he'd known she was already sleeping like a baby.

"You want to practice a little here where it's shallow?" he suggested.

Patty agreed, and he showed her how to adjust the mask and how to breathe, then handed her a pair of flippers to put on her feet. She took off her shorts. She was just wearing her bathing suit, an old navy-blue tank model she liked, but saw that he was going in in his shorts.

Except for swallowing a little saltwater, she got the hang of it right away. The sun was hot and the water—a few degrees cooler than the air temperature—felt good. She paddled around on her stomach for a while, looking down, but there wasn't much to see except rocks and an occasional small fish. She finally went back to the boat, took off the mask and said, "That isn't too exciting."

"What do you want, a shark?"

"That'd be more interesting than rocks."

"We'll go farther out, maybe catch us some conch. There's coral around, too, maybe lobster."

"I wouldn't mind some lobster for dinner," said Patty.

"Yeah, but you wouldn't want to pick them up without gloves on your hands, and I didn't think to bring any."

They climbed back into the boat and he took it farther out where the water was deeper and where she could see larger fish beneath the surface. He told her there were some pretty strong currents and not to swim too far from the boat, then they both put on the gear and jumped overboard.

Patty enjoyed it enormously. She was seeing all kinds of things under the water, and the water was so salty she barely had to do anything to keep afloat. Once in a while Mike would come up to her and point out some fish to her, but most of the time they snorkeled their separate ways.

When she felt her head start to get a little stuffed up, making her wonder whether it had been good for her health even to go in the water, she put the snorkeling equipment into the boat and just floated on her back for a while.

"You had enough?" asked Mike, coming up to her.

"No, I love it out here."

"Ready for a sandwich?"

"Sounds good," she said, then watched as he pulled himself into the boat using just the strength of his arms.

She looked around, then asked, "Where's the ladder?"

"I don't have a ladder."

"How am I supposed to get back in there?"

"Hold onto the side and step on the bottom of the motor."

All Patty saw was about a one-inch piece of metal to step on. She tried, but every time she started to lift herself up, her foot slipped off.

"You having trouble?" Mike asked, looking over the side at her.

"I think you're going to have to tow me in." She felt pretty stupid. She had always considered herself athletic and now she couldn't even get back in a small boat.

"Here, let me show you," he said, jumping back in and coming around to the back. With one easy, fluid motion, he was back in the boat.

She tried it again, and this time was almost in before her foot slipped off and she fell backward, swallowing a lot of water this time and coming up choking.

"I think you have a problem," said Mike, trying rather unsuccessfully not to laugh.

Patty was feeling more and more foolish, but when Mike jumped in again and she felt his hands on her hips in an effort to hoist her up, she was furious. She turned around to tell him to get his hands off her, and the next thing she knew his cold, salty lips were covering hers and she had no way of shoving him away without letting go of the boat and sinking into the water. Instead, she retaliated by keeping her lips firmly pressed together and her eyes wide open and glaring.

He finally broke away and looked at her.

There was a smile on his lips that might have been intended as reassuring or pleasant or any number of things, except that she couldn't control the anger, so the effect was lost. "What'd you do that for?" she wanted to know.

"I couldn't help it. That stubborn mouth of yours just got to me."

"You always go around kissing your enemies, Enfield?"

He moved away from her and trod water. "Hey, I thought we called a truce for today."

"That doesn't make us friends. I just can't believe you did that."

"Listen, it won't happen again, okay? Let's not make such a big deal out of it." He pulled himself easily up into the boat again and, as she watched, made himself comfortable with a sandwich and a Pepsi. That infuriated her out of all proportion. Suddenly she felt ravenous, but she was stuck in the water and looking stupid.

She tried to do what he did and pull herself up with her arms, but halfway up she had to let go.

"That kiss really made you weak, huh?"

"That'll be the day," said Patty, sputtering water.

"You mean you didn't get weak with desire when I kissed you?"

It took real effort, but she managed to ignore him. It was really annoying that he was up in the boat trying to be cute, and she was still in the water wishing she could swim for shore. Only she couldn't swim that far; not even half that far.

Hell, she might've been better off melting in his arms, going with the kiss. Maybe he would have gracefully carried her on board and then she could've insulted him. If she hadn't been feeling so idiotic already, she might have. Kissing him had crossed her mind once or twice during the day. Maybe three times. His tan skin with the bleached hair all over it looked good enough to touch. And she knew what he meant about her mouth, because when he thrust out his own lower lip she got the worst urge to nibble on it. That thought brought her up short by a fresh and unexpected permutation of possibilities.

No, forget that. He was still the enemy, and moreover he was now finished eating and leaning back to light up a cigarette. The perfect picture of the gentleman at ease, while she was hanging on to the boat and watching her skin age right before her eyes. If she stayed in much longer, she was going to look like a shriveled-up old lady.

She looked up at him and saw a downright abnormal gleam in his eyes. Or maybe normal. Using every bit of strength she had, she tried once again to lift herself up. She got far enough to lean her chest over the edge of the boat, but couldn't pull herself up. Just as she was about to let go again, she felt him grab her arms, and then she was being pulled on board—not gracefully, somewhat painfully. But once collapsed on the bottom of the boat she was very happy to be there.

"Thank you," she managed to say ungraciously.

Not a flicker of emotion did Mike display, whatever emotion he might have been feeling.

She waited for him to offer her a sandwich and a drink. When he didn't, she got up and helped herself, then took a seat as far away from him as possible.

He finally said, with elaborate detachment, "You're blaming me again, aren't you? I suppose you think I purposely don't have a ladder on my boat just to give you a hard time. Just like the minute you moved into the alley I hired a band to disturb your sleep. I swear to God, Patty, personal vendettas have never been my style."

All of it was so logical she felt like kicking him.

"You were enjoying yourself, right? We were having a good time. Then, just because you don't happen to have adequate biceps, you get mad at me. Hell, I figured with all that basketball playing, your arms would've been strong enough."

He wasn't making things any better.

"I'll tell you another thing, McIntosh. I bet if any one of the guys in the alley had kissed you, you wouldn't have overreacted like that. Sure, you might have told them where to get off, but you would've been friendly about it. So why the overkill?"

Patty turned her back to him and admired the scenery.

"Hey, it's still Sunday, isn't it? Why don't you just pretend to yourself that I'm not the guy who owns the Honkytonk. Pretend I work at Angelo's. Tomorrow we can go back to being enemies, but I figured when you agreed to go snorkeling you'd leave all that behind for the day."

Damn it! Why did he have to be so reasonable?

"Look, you want to know why I kissed you? Is that what's bugging you? It's because I was beginning to like you, that's why. You're different; I like the way your mind works. Kind of devious, like mine."

Patty turned around. "If I may interrupt this monologue..."

He spread out his arms. "Be my guest."

"I apologize. I felt really stupid not being able to get into the boat. I hate being at a disadvantage like that. It's just me, it's not your fault. I just like to be in control, and I wasn't out there."

"Thank you for being honest with me, Patty, and sharing those thoughts."

"And you can take that smug, self-satisfied smile off your face, too."

He gave a bark of laughter. "I don't suppose you want to do any more snorkeling today."

"You suppose right."

"Want to go up the Keys a little ways? See some of the scenery?"

Her first impulse was to tell him to take her home. But she had to admit that was a childish impulse, so instead she said, "Sure. And if you want to do any more snorkeling, go ahead."

She pulled up the anchor while he started the motor, then went up and took the seat across from his. It had been hot sitting in the boat, but once it was moving the breeze felt wonderful.

SHE WAS SOMETHING ELSE, that Patty McIntosh. He had thought getting to know her a little, maybe getting to be friends, might soften her up, enable him to get his sleeping pattern back to normal. Plus, there was something about her he liked. Usually he didn't like her type on principle, although he'd be hard put to define the principle. He thought it was probably the difference between her and his usual type of woman that he was finding intriguing.

Of course his usual type of woman was the type who hung out in bars, which was how he met them. Since enough women did hang out in bars, and since those types usually were easy game for the owner, he had never had to go looking for a woman. And since he hung out in bars, or at least his bar, that gave them something in common right off.

He didn't figure Patty to hang out in bars. For one thing, she wasn't a drinker, which was sort of peculiar in Key West, but on the other hand it meant she could conduct an intelligible conversation, which was another thing one didn't often come across on the island. Most of the inhabitants either drank or went in for their favorite recreational pharmaceutical, neither of which made for wit or deep thinking of any kind. In fact that was about the only complaint he had against the place. But if he drank enough himself, he usually forgot what he was missing.

All of which was making him feel altogether too philosophical and he decided to try to get things back to where they'd been an hour before. It might not be possible, but it was sure a shame to mess up what had started out to be a great day.

"How old are you, Patty?" he asked, which was a question he generally didn't put to bleached blond singers, but he figured she could handle it.

"Thirty."

"That old? I figured you were younger." He waited for her to ask him his age, and when she didn't, he said, "I'm thirty-four."

That got absolutely no response, so he said, "How come you're not married or something?"

He could tell she had a smart retort all ready, but then she grinned and said, "You sound like my mother."

"Yeah, mine, too. I think parents can't stand to see their kids still enjoying themselves when they were all settled down at that age."

"I like quiet," said Patty.

"Are we back to that?"

She turned to him. "No, that's not what I meant. I was referring to the fact that I grew up with numerous brothers and sisters in a noisy Irish family, and all I want now is a place of my own and quiet."

"I came from a pretty big family, too, but I liked it. I like a lot of people around."

"Which is why you own a bar and why I work at home."

"Well, so far I figure we have absolutely nothing in common." When that got no response, he said, "You have a boyfriend back in Boston?"

"No. I broke up with one before I came down here."

"Yeah? What was he like?"

"Good-looking."

"That's it? Just good-looking?"

"That's it. His one redeeming quality. I seem to go for looks, which is always a mistake."

"You think I'm good-looking?" Mike was almost afraid to ask.

"Yes."

She was more honest than he figured her to be. "You always say what you think?"

"Why not? I think you're sexy, too. But it doesn't mean a thing because I don't like you as a person."

Good-looking and sexy. Well, if he couldn't parlay that combination with her, he was losing his touch. "What do I have to do to get you to like me as a person?"

She glanced over at him. "Replace your band with a chamber quartet."

He had to laugh; she was better with a comeback than anyone he knew. "That's all I have to do to make me Prince Charming, huh?"

"It'd be a start."

He looked over at her while she was looking straight ahead. She might not have the kind of body he preferred, but she was slim and firm, and with the tan she was getting and her hair blowing around in the wind... No, she still wasn't sexy. Cute, yes, but not sexy. Still—and this he couldn't understand—there was something about her mind he was finding sexy. He hadn't known something like that was possible, but right now it wouldn't take any effort at all on his part to reach over and make a second attempt at kissing her. And it had nothing to do with softening her, either.

She turned around and gave him her stubborn look. "Watch where you're going. I don't want to be thrown out of the boat and have to climb in it again."

He chuckled. "All right, Ms. McIntosh. On your right is Big Coppit Key, for one brief moment in history known as Quaalude Key."

"What're you talking about?"

"Oh, that was a few years ago. It seems that one of our local smugglers was bringing in a shipment of 'ludes in his private plane when he was surrounded by DEA helicopters, so he unloaded them all on Big Coppit, two hundred and fifty thousand of them raining down like manna from heaven. It's said the local inhabitants were mellowed out for a full year afterward."

"Is that true?"

"Hell, the place is full of stories like that. Smuggling is a tradition down here."

"I thought that was just Miami."

"Per capita, we've got Miami beat by a mile. I'll tell you another one. About a year and a half ago there was a big shortage of pot in town. Things were getting desperate, at least among those to whom pot is a way of life. So one night the word was out a shipment's coming in. At ten o'clock there was a blackout all over town, lasted until four in the morning. It seems that one of the smuggler's cousins worked at the power plant and arranged it. And during that time half the town was down unloading the shipment."

"Where were the police?"

"Helping them."

"I don't believe it. This seems like a nice town to me."

"Don't you ever read the newspapers?"

"Not since I've been here."

"Well, start reading them. Half the town is on trial and the other half is waiting to be indicted."

"What about you, Mike? Is that what you use this boat for?"

"Not me. The bar makes me more money than I can spend. Anyway, I'm a drinking man. Now if they should bring back Prohibition, you might see me out there."

"But if you did smuggle, you wouldn't tell me anyway."

"That's not necessarily true. The smugglers are well protected down here."

"I hate it. Why do they have to ruin a nice little place like this?"

"They made this place, honey. Hell, most of the people who come down here come because of the freewheeling life-style. Which leads me to my next question: Why did you come down here?"

"My doctor told me to go to a warm climate, and since Key West was farthest south . . ."

"You sick?"

"No. I had pneumonia in Boston, but I feel okay now."

"Maybe I shouldn't have brought you out here."

"Really, I feel fine. Anyway, the water's so warm it couldn't possibly hurt me."

"You aren't using an air conditioner, are you? That could be unhealthy."

"Of course I'm using an air conditioner. It's the only thing that even partially blocks out the noise."

That had been the wrong question to ask. Now she was putting some guilt on him, and he didn't like that. He probably shouldn't have mentioned the smuggling. She was the type who could've lived here for years and never even noticed what was going on around her.

She reached over and put her hand on his arm, which surprised him. "I'm feeling great, really. I'm usually healthy, it's just that I couldn't seem to shake it in Boston with the temperature never going above zero."

Mike slowed down the boat and reached over and put his hand behind her neck, holding her gently. She didn't move, just looked at him with those big eyes, and he decided what the hell, he'd chance it again, and he pulled her head over as he leaned into her, and this time when their lips touched hers were soft and pliable and her eyes at least went to half-mast.

It was a little hard to manage the boat and devote any attention to kissing her, though, so he broke it off before he wanted to and waited for her to yell at him again. He was pretty sure she would since it seemed to be her nature.

When she didn't say anything and the silence began to get to him, he said, "Well, aren't you going to yell at me?"

"Am I that predictable?"

"I just thought—" But he didn't know what he had thought.

Try to figure out women!

DAMN IT, she was beginning to like him. Not just the attraction, but an actual liking. If he had been anyone else but the owner of the Honkytonk Patty would have enjoyed having a relationship with him. Nothing serious, of course—serious meaning permanent—they were too disparate for that, but just a fun thing, an island romance.

But even if they were having the war over the noise, just the fact that he worked nights and slept days and she worked days and slept nights would make it impossible. Still, his band didn't play on Sundays and Mondays. Two days a week wouldn't be bad; any more and it would get too time-consuming anyway.

Patty couldn't figure out his interest. She was sure he had all the women he wanted, so any interest in her had to have an ulterior motive. That brought her back to the subject of their war.

Oh, well, she'd worry about it later. Right now she was enjoying herself and he was amusing company. Of course those stories would've seemed more amusing if that's all they'd been—stories. She didn't like the sound of it if they were true. Boston had its share of crime, but he was making it sound innocent next to Key West. Not that it should affect her personally; she didn't use drugs. She was pretty sure that Nacho and Dirty did, but their types did in Boston, too. And they were still good people and good neighbors to have.

He was turning the boat around now and she asked, "Are we going back?"

"Yeah, we ought to get back before dark. What're you doing tonight?"

"Why?"

"I thought maybe you'd like to come over and go dancing."

"Dancing?"

"Yeah, you know what it is, don't you?"

"At your place?"

"Sure. That's the reason the band plays."

It was slowly sinking in. "But today's Sunday. I thought the band didn't play Sundays and Mondays."

A silence. Then, "They're going to play seven days a week from now on."

"You bastard!"

"Look, if you don't like dancing, just say so."

"I don't believe it. Here you had me thinking I was being unfair with my Greek music, and all along... This was aimed directly at me, right? All your talk of a truce today, and tonight you planned on your little surprise."

He at least had the good sense to look sheepish. "Look, I did it in a moment of anger. I mean, you were playing dirty—"

It was the principle of the thing. Not that she'd hear the music, but he didn't know that. He was determined she wasn't going to get even one night of sleep. "I'll call the police, you know."

"Go right ahead."

"Dancing? You actually thought I'd go dancing with you?"

"Listen, some people do it for enjoyment."

"Some people torture other people for enjoyment."

"And here I thought we were getting along."

"Just don't say another word, all right? Just take me home and don't ever say another word."

An uneasy silence prevailed.

DIRTY AND FRENCHY, both trying to look like innocent tourists and not succeeding, spent the afternoon in Mel Fisher's Treasure Exhibit.

This wasn't as easy as it sounds since the average person could see everything in the museum in under ten minutes.

They didn't do any talking. What they did was walk slowly around, looking at each display of gold and emeralds, generally ignoring the silver and artifacts, and ever so subtly checking out the security of the place.

Afterward they walked in silence to the Green Parrot and discussed over a beer what they had seen.

"Just one security guard," said Frenchy.

"I saw the alarm system, but it'll be out," said Dirty.

"What do we do about the guard?"

"I figure I'll deck him," said Dirty.

"How're you going to see him in the dark?"

"We'll have flashlights. And we'll wear black masks over our faces so he can't pick us out of a lineup."

"Hell, if he gets a look at us at all, he'll pick you out by your hair and your tattoos."

Dirty looked aggrieved. "Don't worry about me, I can disguise myself. Just make sure you wear shoes for once in your life so he can't pick you out."

"How do we get in the cases?"

"Jeez, Frenchy, don't you have no imagination? We take hammers along, that's all. No one's in that area at night to hear the noise, and we got to work fast."

"What's the average blackout, an hour?"

"Sometimes longer, sometimes less. We can figure on a good half-hour at least. I figure ten minutes inside the place would be enough."

"I'm thinking, Dirty, do we have to turn it all over to Nacho?"

Dirty, who'd been thinking the same thing himself but didn't want Frenchy to know it, said, "It's the safest way. What were you planning to do, flash some of that jewelry around town? Let's not be stupid." He wouldn't mind an emerald stud for his ear, though.

"We can't go around spending money, either. Everyone in town knows we don't have any."

Dirty smiled. "I don't figure on staying in town. I have in mind buying a place on one of the smaller Keys, moving in a woman or two—"

"Don't be more stupid than you already are. If you're going to spend like that, you'll have to get out of the Keys altogether. A hit like this is going to get big publicity. I say we leave the country."

"I don't have a passport."

"Get one. Right away. Tomorrow."

"I heard ex-cons can't get passports."

"I didn't know that."

"That's what I heard."

Frenchy thought a moment. "Canada, then. We can get into Canada without a passport."

"Or Mexico. Yeah, Mexico sounds good. I bet we could get Nacho to go along, and he speaks the language. I'll get me a bar on the beach, lie in the sun all day—"

"Yeah, that sounds good. Hell, we can live like kings down there with the peso devalued the way it is."

"The what?"

"Never mind. Just trust me."

Dirty wouldn't trust Frenchy as far as he could kick him.

Frenchy put a cigarette between his yellow teeth and grinned. "I think what I ought to do is move back into Nacho's bathroom for the duration."

"Knuckles is living there."

"What about your bathroom?"

"I don't have a mattress in mine. Listen, Patty's got a chaise on the roof you can sleep on; she'll never know the difference if you're out of there in the morning. When I clean up the alley, you can use my bed."

"Great," said Frenchy, who would welcome a change from his bus. "Come on over with me now and I'll get my stuff."

But Dirty had been eyeing the pool games in progress and decided he'd stick around and hustle. There might not be another blackout for a few weeks and in the meantime he needed to eat.

Chapter Seven

Mike was sitting on the front porch of the Honky-tonk watching the tourists. The women were in shorts and high heels, the men with bellies hanging over the tops of their waistbands and baseball caps on their heads. Most of the men were shirtless, despite the law against it. It wasn't a cruise ship crowd; looked to him like northern Floridians down for the weekend in their pickups or campers.

He felt as though he'd lost something valuable; something he should've been keeping his eye on, but instead looked away for a moment and it was gone. The question was, Could it be recovered?

"What's the matter, Mike?" Knuckles, his baby face showing concern, sat down next to him.

"Listen, Knuckles, you know how to get hold of the band?"

"Yeah, sure—they're staying at Atlantic Shores."

"Call them. Tell them not to come in tonight."

"You can't do that, Mike. They're union, you're going to have trouble."

“Tell ’em they’ll get paid, just not to come in.”

“You’re going to pay them for not playing?” This was something clearly beyond Knuckles’s ability to comprehend.

“That’s right. Tomorrow night, too. We’re going back to five nights a week.”

“This got anything to do with Patty?”

“Why should it have anything to do with Patty?” Mike shouted.

“Jeez, don’t yell at me. I mean, we all saw you take off with her today. How’d it go, huh?”

“I just took her snorkeling, that’s all.”

“That was real friendly of you, Mike.”

Mike gave him a suspicious look. “What’s that supposed to mean?”

“Nothing. Does that mean you no longer think she’s a loony-tune?”

“That’ll depend on the music or lack thereof tomorrow morning.”

Knuckles was nodding. “Yeah, that Greek stuff. I had to put cotton in my ears to get any sleep.”

“Tell me about it.”

“Is that why you’re calling off the band? You make some kind of deal with her?”

“Not yet, but I’m going to try. I want you to take over for me tonight; I’m going out.”

Knuckles, who looked as though he wanted to ask with whom but thought better of it, got off the bar stool. “Yeah, well, I’ll just give the band a call, then.”

Mike figured he was doing the right thing. His arranging with the band to play every night was the same as her blasting out that music in the mornings. Dirty pool, any way you looked at it. Well, he'd play fair if she would. In fact he'd treat her to a nice dinner and try to make up for it.

Although he had a feeling it wasn't going to be all that easy.

PATTY WAS WATCHING the news when the knock came at the door. She opened it and saw Mike standing outside, looking totally different in long pants and a light blue sports shirt. Different, but still good. She debated whether to tell him to get lost, which was what he deserved. But she didn't really feel like it. Since he had taken the initiative and come over, the least she could do was find out why. Anyway, she was glad to see him. "What do you want?" she asked, not wanting to appear to give in to him too easily.

"Could I talk to you for a moment?" He sounded tentative, as though he expected to get the door slammed in his face.

"Just a minute." She closed the front door, closed the bedroom door so he wouldn't be able to see the soundproofing, then opened the front door again and said, "Come on in." She knew she didn't sound gracious, which was fine with her.

He walked in, looking unsure of himself, and she still stood by the door, not wanting him to go any farther. He could say what he had to say and then leave.

"Look, I canceled the band for tonight. I was fighting dirty and I admit it."

Patty realized that now she was the one put back in the position of being guilty, but still she appreciated the gesture. "I suppose that means you expect me to knock off the music tomorrow."

He was starting to smile. "I wouldn't mind. But I didn't come over here to make a deal. I wanted to take you out to dinner."

That explained why he was dressed up. "That's really not necessary."

"I know it's not, I just wanted to. I thought maybe we could go to the Casa Marina, get some lobster."

That was tempting. It probably wouldn't be Maine lobster, but why be fussy. "Well . . ."

"Come on, what'll it hurt? I'll even play you some music on the piano to get dressed by."

Still feeling guilty, but not guilty enough to say no to lobster, she said, "All right, give me ten minutes."

"Take as long as you want."

Patty changed into a white silk dress that was backless and hit her midthigh, put on sandals with heels and added some dangling earrings that glittered when she moved. She knew she was looking as good as she was ever going to look and wondered why she was making the effort for him.

Mike turned around at the piano as soon as she closed the bedroom door, and his reaction was worth the effort. She saw a look in his eyes she had never seen before, and that look told her he was suddenly viewing her differently.

"You don't look like a kid anymore," he said, getting up and coming toward her.

"I'm not a kid."

"Knuckles says you look like someone's kid sister."

"I am someone's kid sister, but I'm not a kid."

"You got to admit sometimes you act like one. There, like that! You ought to see the stubborn look on your face. Just like a little kid."

"You're saying you act like the complete adult?"

He grinned. "No, I've got some kid in me, too, I know that."

Once outside he took her hand and she let him. She could detect watching eyes in the alley, but she didn't care. Let them wonder why the two enemies were now hand in hand. If the geometric progression continued, tomorrow they'd be back to fighting each other.

MIKE COULDN'T FIGURE why he hadn't thought she was sexy before. Just one look at those firm thighs coming out of that silky dress was enough to make his temperature go up ten degrees. And that slim back, bare down to the waist, maybe a little lower, which meant she couldn't be wearing a hell of a lot beneath the dress. She even walked differently. He was going to have to watch the way he acted; he had a feeling that if he made a move on her too soon, he'd blow it.

Although what it was he'd blow, he wasn't sure. He wasn't even sure how he felt about her anymore. All he knew was he was looking forward to the dinner with her more than he'd looked forward to anything with a woman for a long time.

There was a taxi out in front of the Honkytonk and they took it to the Casa Marina. It wasn't his kind of place, a little too pretentious. But the kind of places he felt comfortable in probably wouldn't appeal to Patty. She had class, and the Casa Marina was the classiest place in town.

He could see right away she was impressed by the Spanish architecture, but when they walked inside and she got a load of the opulent lobby, she turned to him and grinned.

"You trying to impress me, Enfield?"

"I didn't succeed, huh?"

"If the food's good, you're forgiven. I'm just glad I put a dress on."

He was glad she had, too, but he didn't say so.

They had a twenty-minute wait to be seated, so he took her into the bar and asked her what she'd have to drink.

"I feel like I should say Perrier in here, but I'll be damned if I will. I'll have a tomato juice."

"Anything in it?" Hoping, but without much hope. He just shrugged when she shook her head. It wasn't that he cared whether she drank or not; it was just that it made him feel like a bigger drinker than he was to be the only one drinking.

There was a live band, which he thought she might object to, but she didn't say anything, leading him to wonder if it was only his band she didn't like. "Wanna dance?" he asked.

"Walking in these shoes is about all I can manage."

It was a shame. He wouldn't mind getting close to her on the dance floor. He knew half the people in the bar, and most of them stopped by to say hello. He introduced Patty each time, and after each one left he gave her a capsule description of the person. He left out a few pertinent details about some of them, but she'd never know the difference.

"You know everyone in town," she said at one point.

"Stay here long enough and so will you. Other than the tourists, just about everyone knows everyone else."

"And each other's business?"

"That, too. They'll be talking about us tomorrow."

"I don't think I like that."

"Why not? All we're doing is having dinner together."

"And if we weren't?"

He smiled. "Then we'd be a little more discreet."

"How do you manage being discreet in Key West?"

"Usually by going to Miami. Why, you in the mood for a trip up the Keys tonight?"

"I'm just in the mood for dinner."

He chuckled. "Maybe the lobster will soften you up."

"Maybe it will, but not enough to get me to Miami."

"Then we'll throw discretion to the winds and just stay here."

She laughed at that, surprising him. She didn't seem to be taking anything wrong tonight. Either that or she was feeling the same way he was. Well, what the hell, she had said she found him sexy, hadn't she?

They'd have a good dinner and maybe he'd be able to talk her into having some wine with it. He was fairly confident civilized people in Boston drank wine with their meals. He'd take her back to her place, maybe play a little romantic music on the piano, prolong the suspense for a while. Then—

"You have a devious expression on your face, Mike. What're you thinking about?"

He put his arm around her shoulders. "You wouldn't believe me if I told you."

"Try me."

"I was thinking about your piano."

"My piano?"

"I told you you wouldn't believe me."

He could swear she looked disappointed.

HE WAS WALKING HER to her door and had the expression of a man who figured he'd struck out. Mike seemed to have some notion that the only way to soften up a woman was to get her drunk. Once she had refused—for the third time—the offer of wine with their dinner, he had seemed to change. It was as though he thought if she wouldn't have a drink with him, she wasn't about to have anything else, either.

That idea was patently ridiculous. Patty had enjoyed his company all evening. The meal was excellent, as was the conversation, and she could see no good reason for the evening to end so soon.

He stood beside her as she opened the door, and when she asked him if he wanted to come in, he paused only a second before saying, "I didn't think you'd ask."

"I'm sorry I can't invite you in for a drink, but I don't have any liquor."

He followed her into the apartment. "I don't have to drink, you know."

She closed the door and leaned against it. "Neither do I, although I have the feeling you think it's some kind of prerequisite."

She saw the smile forming on his lips, then he was leaning over, his arms going around her, and she was moving away from the door and into his arms. It was far sexier kissing him standing up than it had been in the boat, feeling his body moving slowly in on her, hers moving, too, until they couldn't get any closer. And then his mouth, moving around, taking control of hers, and the feelings stirring inside of her that were partly trepidation and partly anticipation.

When he finally broke off the kiss, he said, "I'd ask you if you know what you're doing, only you're dead sober so I assume you do."

She smiled. "I'm only taking advantage of the truce. It is still in effect, isn't it?"

"And here I was thinking I was the one taking advantage of it."

Mike took her hand and led her into the living room, and she watched him as he surveyed the three chairs and chaise longue and, for the first time, seemed to note the absence of a couch. He finally made up his mind and sat down on the chaise, pulling her down beside him. He leaned back, and she went with him, and then they were kissing again and his hand was moving slowly up and down her bare back, which gave her all kinds of lovely sensations, the feel of his skin against hers even more erotic than the feel of the silk against her bare skin had felt all night.

When his hand slowly moved inside the dress and around to the front to cup one of her breasts, she gave a murmur of enjoyment and shifted around to give him more room. He pulled her back, pulling her half on top of him, and at the same time his tongue was prying open her lips and his other hand was on one thigh and she felt encompassed by him and a little dizzy and she was wondering at the extent to which she was feeling carried away, which wasn't like her, and then she told herself to quit analyzing the situation and just enjoy it.

She was at the point where she was wishing this could go on forever when he pulled her up so that they were both half sitting, and said, "Couldn't we continue this in the bedroom?"

She was just about to say "What a good idea" when she remembered what there was in the bedroom that she didn't want him to see, and with the greatest feeling of regret, she said, her voice somewhat shaky, "No, I don't think so, Mike."

She could feel the immediate tension in him. "I do think so."

Trying to pull her emotions together, she sat all the way up and looked at him. "I'm sorry."

"I don't believe this. Thirty years old and you're still a tease?"

"Is that all you're interested in?" She hated saying that, but it was the only thing that came to mind.

He just looked at her for a moment. "No, that's not all I'm interested in. If it were, it wouldn't be you I would take to dinner. But just for the record, if I'm not mistaken, lady, it was all you were interested in about two seconds ago."

Not able to meet his eyes, she got up and pulled down her dress. "Actually, Mike, it's past my bedtime."

"Good. Let's go to bed."

"I don't think you understand."

"You're right, I don't. Now why don't you quit playing games, Patty, and let's get back to where we were a minute ago."

He got up and was heading in the direction of her bedroom. She moved around him quickly, blocking the way. "No, Mike—not tonight."

He tried to pull her to him, but she resisted. "What happened, Patty? What happened that I didn't notice?"

"Nothing. It's been a lovely evening and I've enjoyed it. I just think we ought to end it now."

"It's only eleven o'clock."

"That's when I go to bed."

He suddenly relaxed and smiled down at her. "I tell you what. Give me five minutes to change your mind, and if I don't, I'll leave." He tried to move past her to the bedroom, but she blocked his way, feeling pretty silly holding her arms across the door frame.

"What is it with you? Your bedroom a mess or something, is that it? Listen, you ought to see my place."

"No, it's not a mess," she said. Then something must have shown in her face because he yanked her away from the door and pulled it open in one swift movement.

He stood for a second looking into the dark, shaking his head. He reached for the light switch and the overhead light went on. There was a stunned silence, then he said, "Soundproofing?" He couldn't believe it.

She walked away from him but he grabbed her by the arm and pulled her back. "All this time you've had a soundproof room and you've been driving me crazy with that lousy music?"

"I haven't had it that long."

"And you weren't going to tell me about it, were you? You were going to go on letting me believe I was disturbing your sleep, making me feel so guilty I paid the band not to play tonight. And all the time...all the time..."

"I'm sure whatever you had to pay the band didn't cost as much as that damn soundproofing."

He gave her a frightening look. "I wasn't complaining about the cost."

She stood there, feeling guilty and not knowing what to say.

"So what was the point of that whole little seduction scene? The dress, half naked beneath it. Inviting me in. The scene on the chaise. What were you trying to accomplish? Whatever it was, it was unnecessary. Whether you know it or not, I was starting to have real feelings for you."

"It wasn't a seduction scene."

He turned a look on her so hostile she felt herself shrink. "Then why is it I feel I was taken?" he asked, then went to the front door and opened it, not saying another word as he went out and slammed the door behind him.

DIRTY WAS JUST COMING OUT of Nacho's apartment when he saw Patty's door open, the light spilling out, then saw Mike come out and slam it behind him. Dirty ducked back in and shut the door.

"Guess what I just seen?" he said.

"Around here, it could be anything," said Nacho.

"Mike just come out of Patty's."

"Yeah? I wonder how he made out."

"Not so good, judging by the way he slammed the door."

"I didn't figure Patty to be a pushover," said Nacho.

"I think they're good together," said Dirty.

"What's he need her for, he's already got money," Frenchy chimed in. "People like them ought to distribute the wealth."

"That's communism," said Nacho.

"It's equality," argued Frenchy.

"I like the sound of it, whatever it is," said Dirty. Not that he had any intention of distributing his own money when he got it. The first thing he was going to do when he got to Mexico was buy himself a white double-breasted suit and a Panama hat, maybe get himself a gold watch, have one of the emeralds made into an earring, and . . .

"What are you going to do with your share, Dirty?" asked Frenchy, as though reading his mind.

"Invest it."

"Yeah, right. Me, I'm going to buy a yacht and sail around the world," said Frenchy. "With an all-female crew."

"What about you?" Dirty asked Nacho.

"I'm going to get me a cattle ranch. I might even get married and settle down."

"Not you," said Dirty.

"Why not?"

Dirty grinned. "Because you can't ride a horse drunk."

"I can do anything drunk," said Nacho.

"The important thing," said Frenchy, "is to live the way we always have for a few months. What I think is, we say we're going to take a little trip in my bus, maybe just up the Keys."

"And then hello Mexico," said Dirty.

They all liked the sound of that.

DEAR DEIRDRE,

I swear, Deirdre, if I ever mention another man to you, ignore me. I am going to go off men permanently.

This is a new Patty talking. Men are stupid, insufferable, annoying, etc., etc., etc. Went out with Mike tonight, that's my enemy from next door, and it ended disastrously. And the worst of it is, I think I'm falling in love.

That's a shock, right? Me in love? Well, it's not too late to fall back out of love, I hope, and I'm going to make a concerted effort to do just that. Listen, just ignore all this; I'll probably be back to normal in the morning. Right now, though, I'm too frustrated to sleep and writing to you is cheaper than going to a shrink.

I'm going to hell down here in Key West, Deirdre. You know what I almost did tonight? I almost went to bed with a guy on a first date. Which we always agreed was a big mistake, right? Well, all Mike had to do was touch me and my control was shattered. I guess there's a first time for everything, but it sure surprised me. The only thing that stopped me was the soundproofing, which I know sounds off the wall, but it's a long story and I don't feel like going into it now. Suffice it to say, my deviousness backfired on me.

I have an idea. Why don't you take off from work and come down here? I need someone sane and sensible around, and since I don't know anyone sane and sensible, you're the next best thing.

Maybe I should just come back to Boston. This place is as pretty as a picture and the weather is wonderful, but it's corrupt to the core, if you can believe it. Not Mike, he's one of the few honest people around. At least I think he is.

Oh, hell, I'm rambling on and probably boring you to death, but there's no one here I can talk to. Call me when you get this—collect if you want—and I'll clue you in on the latest episodes of the continuing soap opera I've gotten myself into.

And see a Celtics game for me, okay?

Love,
Patty

Chapter Eight

Patty spent the next week ignoring Mike.

She did this in a number of ways. She would have dispensed with the basketball practice, only her neighbors wouldn't let her. Dirty and Nacho would arrive every morning ready for a game, and sometimes even Knuckles stayed up for it.

She stopped the piano practice. Playing the piano reminded her of Mike anyway, and by her not playing he would get the message that she had better things to do than continue the feud.

In her effort to ignore him, she did manage to walk by the Honkytonk several times a day. She had to pass it in order to get to the Pier House beach. Then she found that the Pier House market sold a number of delectables, and she took to doing her shopping there. It was more expensive than Fausto's, but she convinced herself it was worth it.

And of course there were numerous shops on that end of Duval that she wanted to check out, which meant passing the Honkytonk a few more times.

Since she was ignoring him, she never glanced to her side when she passed so she didn't really know whether he was aware she was ignoring him or not.

When a week had passed and he still hadn't spoken to her, she came to the conclusion that ignoring him hadn't been one of her better strategies.

Somewhere in her subconscious she knew that the best strategy would be to apologize to him for not telling him about her soundproofing. She preferred to listen to her conscious rather than her subconscious, though, because her conscious told her she'd feel stupid apologizing to him, and she didn't want to feel stupid. She also didn't like apologizing.

She told herself that one of these days she'd grow up and begin to be attracted to men for their better qualities instead of their looks. When she was younger she had thought it would be nice to go with a guy who had something in common with her. Later, though, at MIT and then for the short time she worked for IBM, she came to the conclusion that men with something in common with her were bores. It wasn't that she didn't enjoy discussing general relativity and quantum physics, it was just that it didn't make for a very scintillating discussion. It was mostly just a matter of each spouting his or her own theory, then trying to defend it. And the end of the evening found her going home alone, because conversation aside, she wasn't attracted to that kind of man. She found them singularly unsexy.

When she found she could make more money at home devising math and physics software, with some games on the side, she said farewell to male mathematical geniuses and begin making forays into the real world of Boston, which meant the singles bars, where, invariably, she was smitten by some man's looks and just as invariably ended up bored to death by him.

It wasn't that Mike couldn't turn out to be the same. It was just that she didn't think he would. Granted she hadn't spent much time with him, but the time they had spent together hadn't been spent with her listening to him talking about his work. She'd heard enough about law and accounting and the field of medicine in Boston to last her a lifetime. Most men only wanted to talk about their work; she wanted to talk about everything but work.

Mike had been both interesting and entertaining. He hadn't been deeply philosophical, but that was an asset. She could be deeply philosophical on her own time; she didn't require a man along for that. What he had been was good-looking and fun and sexy, and she didn't see any reason why she had to aspire to anything more than that. That was the perfect combination in a man and up until now she hadn't met a man with all three qualities.

She felt it would not be in her best interests to make the first move. Since Mike wasn't making that move, however, she let herself be talked into going down to The Bull with Dirty and Nacho one night where they endeavored to teach her to shoot pool. She found she had no natural aptitude for the game and quickly lost interest, leaving Dirty and Nacho free to hustle the customers.

They had introduced her to a few men in the bar and one of them, Sam, turned out to be interesting and with a good sense of humor, and when he asked her if she wanted to walk down to Two Friends to hear some jazz, she readily agreed. She only hoped Mike noticed her walking by the Honkytonk in the company of a man.

Unlike most of her neighbors' acquaintances, Sam had a visible means of support, being down in Key West to get a contract with the navy for his chemical company. Patty made an effort to enjoy his company, and for a few dates that was possible. Along about the second week of seeing him, though, she broke it off abruptly. The natural progression of dating had reached the point where now it was time for sex, and her feelings for him were decidedly asexual. It was partly that he wore hair spray on his thinning hair and partly his voice, high and with the same quality as fingernails across a blackboard. In any event, he was all right for a friend, but she aspired to more.

What Patty aspired to was seeing Mike again, and it began to seem it wouldn't be possible unless she was the one to unbend and seek him out.

That went against the grain, but like any good mathematical equation, there was a natural progression, and in this one the next step had to be hers.

MIKE WAS ANGRY for about twenty-four hours, then he began to see the humor in the situation. He knew if the scene had been in a movie with the guy working up to get the girl into the bedroom, and with it ending that she'd had the bedroom soundproofed, he would have laughed his head off. He knew if he recounted the evening to anyone, any of his friends, they'd be falling off their bar stools with laughter. So she had been devious, so what? He was capable of being just as devious, and he admired the way her mind worked.

On the other hand, she was now in the wrong and he was in the right and the next move had to come from her.

Her little walks by the Honkytonk each day didn't go unnoticed by him, nor did the fact that she made it a point never to look his way. When this happened, Knuckles would usually nudge him and say, "That's the third time today," or maybe the fourth or fifth.

He had also noticed the cessation of the piano playing. Either that or she was keeping the noise down. In any case, he appreciated it. The basketball practice he was learning to live with, and it never lasted more than a half-hour anyway.

The first thing Mike did when he saw Patty walking by the Honkytonk in the company of another man was order a shot of tequila, even though it was pretty early for him to start drinking; the second thing he did was say to Nacho, who was seated beside him, "Who's the guy with Patty?"

Nacho immediately looked slightly uncomfortable. "That's Sam. He hangs out at The Bull."

"What'd you do, set her up with him?"

"Nothing like that. She was down there with us one night and happened to meet him. He's a nice guy, Mike."

"He looks like he uses hair spray."

Nacho laughed a little too hard at that. "I don't think it's anything serious. It's probably like you and those singers."

If there was one thing he didn't want it to be like, it was that. Still, it hadn't looked to him like there was anything sexual between them. They had been holding hands, sure, but they looked more like a couple of friends than anything else.

"He spend the night over there?" he asked Nacho.

"Not that I've noticed, and I would've noticed. Patty's got this schedule, she's in bed every night at eleven. Alone."

Mike hoped it stayed that way.

He couldn't help noticing that Patty was looking more and more like a native. When she had first arrived she had all kinds of outfits she paraded out in, but now she seemed to have settled for the cotton gym shorts, T-shirt and sneakers that just about everyone in Key West wore. It didn't matter if you were eighty and three hundred pounds, that was the only way to dress in the tropics. It made the natives look like a bunch of overgrown kids, particularly since most of them rode bikes.

The only thing that didn't look native about her was her deep tan. The residents left the tans to the tourists, with the exception of the fishermen who were out on their boats all the time. She was looking good. Healthy. That had never been something he looked for in a woman, but he appreciated it in Patty. To tell the truth, he still hadn't figured out why he was attracted to her. All he knew was ever since the night he'd taken her to the Casa Marina and it had ended in a disaster, he hadn't looked at another woman. Well, maybe looked, but he hadn't done anything else.

When the day came that Mike noticed Patty was once again alone, he said to Dirty, "What happened to the boyfriend?"

"You talking about Patty?"

"Quit trying to be cool, Dirty."

"I don't know, Mike. All I know is he was down at The Bull drowning his sorrows last night. I would guess she broke it off."

He decided to give her another week, and if she didn't make her move, he was going to have to do it himself. It went against the grain, but the wait was becoming frustrating.

MIKE WAS SITTING out on the porch of the Honkytonk when he saw Patty coming his way with a purposeful look about her, and the purpose appeared to be him. "Get lost," he said to Knuckles, who seemed to catch on to the situation with more alacrity than usual, and vacated his seat to go inside.

Patty stepped up on the porch and sat down next to him, which was rather surprising. He was wondering whether sitting next to him constituted a move or whether she also had to say something. Now that she was seated, she was staring straight ahead and appeared to have lost her voice. He gave her about thirty seconds more of silence, then said, "Buy you a drink?"

"I'll have a Coke, thank you." There was no emotion of any kind in her voice.

He turned around to the bar and got them each a drink, and when he set the Coke in front of her she leaned over the straw and drank it all down until all she got was a slurping noise. He was impressed. He had never seen anyone chug-a-lug a Coke before. She either had to be real nervous or real thirsty.

"Nice day," he said to her, by way of being pleasant.

She ignored the pleasantry.

"Seen the latest T-shirts around?" he asked, hoping for a communications breakthrough. He was referring to the I SURVIVED THE BUBBA BUST TRIAL shirts, but either she hadn't heard of them or she didn't care one way or the other.

He lit a cigarette and slowly blew out the smoke. "I'll make it easy on you, Patty. I accept your apology."

Her stubborn look appeared so fast he almost laughed. "I didn't hear myself apologize."

"That's just it; I was saving you the effort."

"I don't see why I should be the one to always apologize."

"Maybe because you're the one who's always wrong."

She shot off the bar stool and he had to reach out and grab her arm to stop her from leaving. "Hey, I'm only giving you a hard time. Sit down and we'll discuss the cease-fire."

She still looked just as stubborn and not a bit amenable, so he put a whole lot of sincerity into his voice and said, "I missed you."

She didn't exactly melt at the words, as he had hoped, but she relaxed the muscles in the arm he was holding and changed her stubborn look to one of doubt.

"I mean it, Patty. And if you hadn't stopped by tonight, I wouldn't have held out much longer." Mike was being nice, but letting her know at the same time that she had been the one to give in first.

A fighting gleam came into her eyes and she sat back down on the bar stool. "You talk like it's all been a game, Mike."

"Well, hasn't it been? We've been playing games with each other right from the start."

"I don't see it that way."

"Sure you do, you're just like me. You like games of strategy."

"I don't know what you're talking about."

Mike chuckled. "You think I haven't heard how you've been hustling those high school kids over at the Atari place?"

"I didn't take money from them."

"You hustled them, just the same."

"I hear all you hustle is female singers."

That must've been Dirty and his big mouth. "Yeah, but I don't take money from them." He had thought that was pretty humorous, but she seemed annoyed now, so he said, "Hey, I was only kidding. The only females I hustle are ladies from Boston."

"Is that what you're trying to do? Hustle me?"

"Actually, I was just trying to get you to talk. And I succeeded. So now that we have your apology out of the way, how about having dinner with me? I got a new chef, he'll fix us up something special."

"I still didn't apologize."

"Sure you did, in your own way."

Dirty and Nacho walked by, did a double take when they saw Mike with Patty, then continued on their way, big grins splitting their faces. He looked around and saw Knuckles, also grinning happily, and told him to tell the chef to put on two steaks to broil.

"How do you know I want a steak?" Patty asked him.

"Don't you?"

"Yes, but you could've asked." She seemed ready to start a fight at the slightest provocation, making him wonder if things would ever be smooth between them.

THEY ATE DINNER. They argued the relative merits of rare steak (hers) and well-done (his), baked potatoes with butter (her preference) versus baked potatoes with sour cream and chives (his preference), and whether Key lime pie was better with meringue or whipped cream. Patty argued on the side of whipped cream even though she preferred meringue, just to be perverse. And also because Mike was fun to argue with.

Over his second cup of coffee and her second cup of tea, though, Mike's employees started interrupting them almost continuously until Mike finally said, "I guess I better get to work, Patty, but I'm real happy you came by. Stick around if you want and listen to the band."

His suggestion practically left her speechless. Stick around and listen to the band she had paid good money to avoid hearing? Still, it was early, and unless she wanted to lock herself in her soundproof room at nine at night, she was going to have to listen to the band if she went home, so instead she strolled down Duval and saw Nacho in The Bull shooting pool and went inside to watch.

Nacho winked at her, finished the game in a flurry of banked shots, then took the proffered drink from the loser and joined Patty at one of the tables.

"Hey, I saw you and Mike together. It on again?"

Patty shrugged. "We're speaking."

"Play it close to the chest, I don't believe you anyway. Listen, we all think you'd be good for Mike."

"Good for him? What do you mean, like vitamins?"

Nacho grinned. "A steadying influence. Mike's not like me and Dirty. He could do with a good woman."

"And you think what I need is a bar owner?"

"Mike's a good guy, Patty; he's there when you need him, you know what I mean?"

"No."

Nacho, a few rum and Cokes no doubt flowing through his system, got a maudlin look on his face and tone to his voice. "He's like a brother, you know? He's bailed me out of jail a few times. Dirty, too."

"What were you in jail for?"

Nacho's eyes went wide with innocence. "Nothing bad, Patty—just a few fights. Drunk and disorderly's all it was."

Patty, thinking she could learn just about anything about Mike from Nacho in his present condition, said, "Well, since I don't get drunk and disorderly, what do I need him for?"

"The Honkytonk makes him good bucks, you know."

"I don't want his money."

"Well, yeah, I mean you got bucks of your own. What I can tell you is he'll be straight with you. He's honest. One of the few honest men I know."

Patty thought about his devious maneuvers, then thought about her own, and didn't argue the point. "What's his record with women?" she wanted to know.

Nacho gave her an ingratiating look. "Well, if you want to know the truth, Patty, show Mike a blonde with boobs and—" Her expression must have clued him in because he instantly said, "I'm sorry I said that, Patty, it just slipped out. I try to watch my language around you, but—"

"Relax, Nacho, I know what boobs are. So if that's the type he goes for, why the interest in me?"

"I swear to God, none of us can figure it out. Hey, not that we don't all think you're great, but Mike's doing something we've never seen him do before—he's going for class."

Patty, who would just as soon have had boobs rather than class, didn't say anything.

"I think Mike likes you for the same reason we like you. We can talk to you. Most of those bimbos he goes for can't string together two sentences. They might be all right in the sack, but, Jeez, Patty, you gotta excuse my language. I keep forgetting I'm talking to a lady."

Patty, who had heard worse language on the public transportation in Boston any day of the week, didn't even know why he was apologizing. "Has he ever been married?" she asked him.

"Mike? Not that I know of. He's had a few live-ins, but none of them have lasted long. But that's Key West, Patty; nothing down here lasts too long."

That was an immediate challenge to Patty. She wanted to be the one that did last. Unless she was mistaken, Mike was just the kind of man she had long been looking for.

And to think she'd always made fun of the "boy next door" mentality.

PATTY SPENT AN HOUR with Mike here and there during the week when their schedules permitted. One afternoon he took her out in his boat, another time they went bike riding and most evenings she ate dinner with him at the Honkytonk.

When he mentioned taking her out on Sunday night, she suggested he come over to her place for dinner instead, and by the gleam in his eyes saw he got the message. Boat rides and bike rides were fine, but she wanted more than just friendship with Mike.

She told him to come by at eight, and by then the meat loaf and baked potatoes were done, the salad made, and Rachmaninoff was playing on the stereo.

At eight-thirty he called and said he'd be over in a few minutes.

"I had dinner ready at eight," she informed him, slightly miffed.

"This is Key West, Patty—no one's ever on time."

"I am," she said.

"Well, you'll have to learn to go with it. This is the tropics, you know."

Patty, who was not only never late but usually early, was tired of everyone's excuses. Living on an island or living in the tropics seemed to be an excuse for anything, she had found. An inability to be where you were supposed to be when you were supposed to be was only one annoyance. When the bank machines didn't work, it was blamed on the tropics. When her computer broke down, it was blamed on the tropics, even though she kept her apartment air-conditioned. The high incidence of alcoholism was blamed on island living.

Now the fact that she had prepared dinner on time and it was slowly drying out was being blamed on the tropics.

Annoyed, Patty changed from the sundress she had been wearing into her usual shorts, and went outside to shoot a few baskets and let off some steam.

She was shooting a basket when Mike arrived and didn't hear his approach. When he put his arms around her and kissed her neck, causing her a moment's dizziness, she decided to blame that reaction on the tropics, too. A kiss in Boston had never made her dizzy.

The dinner turned out all right after all. "Meat loaf," said Mike, when she served him, sounding neither negative nor positive.

"I thought I'd fix something you don't have at the Honkytonk."

"Haven't had meat loaf in years." He took a bite, smiled, said, "This is different, I like it. What's in it, anyway?"

"Trying to steal my recipe?"

"No, just curious."

"I fix it with Lipton Onion Soup mix."

"Yeah? Well, it's great."

Patty hoped the dinner conversation wasn't going to revolve around her cooking. Cooking was maybe the least of her talents and didn't interest her much.

But when Mike said, "I've been thinking about this a lot, you know," she wished he'd go back to talking about her cooking.

"What do you mean?" she asked, knowing very well what he meant.

"Seeing you again; being with you. We've wasted a lot of time."

"We would've wasted less if you'd been on time for dinner."

He started to laugh. "You were in that much of a hurry to get me alone, huh?"

"Keep it up, Mike."

He was still laughing. "I love it. Now I'm getting threatened. Listen, you think I'm not in a hurry? I've been patiently waiting while you went out with this one and that one—"

"I went out with one guy, that's all."

"Yeah, the one with the hair spray."

She had just taken some potato in her mouth, and now started to laugh and choked on it. She grabbed for her glass of water, drank some to stop the choking, then said, "I didn't know I was being watched."

"You were being watched."

"He was a nice guy."

"I'm sure he was. Nice and dull, right?"

Which had been the truth. Sam had refused to get into an argument about anything, saying arguing raised his blood pressure. Wanting to change the subject, she said, "I have ice cream for dessert. Chocolate marshmallow or raspberry sherbet."

"That's not what I want for dessert." He was getting up out of his chair and walking around the table. "And don't give me any nonsense about cleaning up first, either," he said, taking her hands and pulling her up out of her chair.

"But we just ate," she started to protest.

"That's swimming you aren't supposed to do on a full stomach. We're not going to swim." He then effectively cut off any further argument by kissing her, which hadn't even been necessary because she'd been through arguing at that point anyway.

MIKE WAS LOOKING around the room, not paying any attention to her. "I feel like I'm in a padded cell," he finally said.

Patty knew the feeling. "You want me to open the door?"

"Yeah, would you?"

She got out of bed and opened the door. "Is that better?"

"A little. Don't you feel locked up in here?"

"It's better than feeling bombarded by music."

"Let's not get into that. Come on over here."

Back in bed, he leaned over her and she put her arms around him, pulling him close. She saw his eyes moving to the side and said, "Close your eyes and you won't even notice it."

"But then I won't be able to see you."

"Then look at me and quit looking at the walls."

"You're right, it's just a little strange is all. I'll get used to it." He began to kiss her, slowly, lingeringly, stopping every so often to break away and look at her and say things like, "You were worth waiting for, you know that?" and, "We should have had our heads examined to wait this long."

Once they began to make love, Patty didn't think anyone was noticing the walls. He was an amazing lover, so good it was almost as though he had been programmed to her needs. What's more, she could tell he was thoroughly enjoying himself, not the serious kind of lover who acts dedicated to the cause but never really lets loose and has fun. And because he was that way, she found herself shedding all inhibitions and really going with it, which wasn't her usual way.

Afterward, when she was getting back her breath and Mike was lighting a cigarette, he said, "You were really enthusiastic."

Embarrassed that he might have thought she overdid it, she got defensive. "You were pretty enthusiastic yourself."

"Hey, I wasn't complaining. I'm just saying I thought you were great, that's all."

Patty turned her face into his chest. "I don't usually get that carried away." Meaning, of course, that she usually didn't care that much.

"Hell, neither do I. We're good together, you know that?"

She thought they were better than good together, she thought they made a perfect combination.

MIKE STAYED THE NIGHT. It was the best night's sleep he'd had in ages, if you could discount the times they both awoke and made love again, and he certainly wasn't going to discount that.

Patty in bed had been like an advanced course in "How to Get the Most Enjoyment Out of Your Sex Life." She was sweet and soft and sensual and athletic and assertive and animalistic all mixed up together, and that mixture did more for the sex they had than the Lipton Onion Soup mix did for the meat loaf. Whatever she had, no woman he had previously met could come near it. His only worry now was that by some kind of osmosis the entire male population of the town would sense what he had found and go after Patty. He was determined to keep her all for himself.

That was pure camouflage, of course, and he was honest enough with himself to admit it. It wasn't just the sex, it was her. Or, more correctly, his feelings for her. For one thing, he was feeling possessive, and that was something new. He wasn't going to call it love—he'd be damned if he was going to call it love—but it sure as hell was the next thing to it.

The soundproofing, once he got used to the feeling of being in a padded cell, was wonderful, too. He did hear Patty get up before him the next morning, but once she left the bedroom he didn't hear a sound, even though, as he found out later, she had played basketball right against the bedroom's outside wall. He briefly thought of soundproofing his own place, but then he had a better idea. It would be cheaper and more fun if he could somehow get Patty to let him move in with her. And besides, living alone no longer seemed so wonderful. What would really be wonderful would be having Patty around all the time.

He didn't figure that was going to be easy. She wasn't any kid, and guys before him had probably tried for the same thing. And he knew they hadn't succeeded because she'd told him she had never lived with a guy.

What it was going to call for was some strategy on his part. As it was, the only times they could be together for any length of time were Sunday and Monday nights. If he could make their times together good enough, wouldn't she want more? And the only way to see more of each other was if they were living together.

And, of course, there was always the old play-on-their-sympathy ploy. He could plead lack of sleep, maybe hint around to use her bedroom. He thought it was too soon to mention living together; he didn't want to scare her off.

Hell, there were probably a million ideas he could come up with. He'd just have to think on it awhile.

Chapter Nine

Two weeks after her first night with Mike, spring break descended on Key West and, along with it, thousands of boisterous, drunken college students who staked a claim to her block of Duval Street and made venturing outdoors a risky business.

Overcast skies didn't help matters. The students, who would normally spend their days at the beach, now spent all day in and out of the Honkytonk and Sloppy Joe's and Captain Harry's. In her opinion, she had seen little enough of Mike before; now she saw virtually nothing of him.

"I don't want you to take this personally," he told her, "but the bands always play every night during spring break. Ask anyone. It's our best business all year. And I've got to be around because these kids get into a lot of trouble."

She believed him, but she didn't like it. Most of the police in town were now centered on the 200 block of Duval, along with every hooker, small-time drug dealer and many of the town's high school students who were hoping to pass for college age.

Except for emergency trips to the grocery store, Patty didn't venture out at all. When Mike had a few minutes, he'd stop by, but there was never any time to do anything more than hold a brief conversation. Patty tired of brief conversations very quickly.

The only excitement in her life during that first week of spring break was when Dirty got thrown into jail for starting a fight with one of the college kids, sending the kid to the hospital with six stitches in his head.

Since the fight had taken place in the Honkytonk, Mike was angry and refused to bail him out. Nacho came by to see her and begged her to bail out Dirty.

"I think he deserves to be in jail," Patty told him. "He could've killed that kid."

"You know Dirty," said Nacho. "He's the gentlest man around when he's sober. He just gets crazy when he drinks, that's all. It's not his fault."

"He doesn't have to drink, does he?"

"Patty, Dirty's going to go crazy in that jail cell. You'll see, he won't touch a drink for months after this. Anyway, I was there and the kid started the fight." Nacho was using his wheedling voice. It was rather breathy, full of sincerity, and along with this his eyes took on an innocent look. She had long since learned this was the voice he used when he wanted to con someone.

Since she liked Dirty, though, and really didn't want to see a friend of hers in jail, she went with Nacho to see Billy Boyd, the bail bondsman, and got Dirty out.

Dirty was properly contrite for about ten minutes. Then he launched into the scheme he had thought up in jail so that when his sentencing came up, he'd get off with probation.

"What I figure," Dirty told them, "is I'll get my hair cut, put myself in the rehab center for a week, catch a few AA meetings, and when I have to go to court I'll have all this evidence to show I've cleaned up my act. Hell, I might even get a part-time job."

Patty wished he'd do all those things for real, but she didn't offer her opinion.

"They feed you good in the rehab place," said Nacho. "And they got color TV."

"Yeah," said Dirty, really getting into it now, "and I hear you meet lots of women at the AA meetings."

"I'll just be glad when spring break is over," Patty said to them. "These kids are driving me nuts. I get asked to dance just walking through the alley."

"You got about six more weeks of it to go through," said Nacho.

"What?" she said, hoping he was kidding. "I thought spring break was a week."

"Not anymore. They stagger the break now. Right now what we're getting are some of the Southern colleges."

That news didn't make her day.

"Way to go, Dirty," said Nacho, as soon as Patty had left them. "There could be a blackout anytime with the weather the way it's been, and you might've been in jail."

"I swear, Nacho, I couldn't help myself. You'd have done the same thing."

"Not in front of a cop I wouldn't."

"Anyway, it was worth it. I got this great idea when I was in jail."

Dirty and his great ideas. "Yeah? What's this one?"

"Listen to this. I know how you are when you're drunk, and I'm not much better. I mean we're both capable of getting into fights, but that's about all we're capable of. And everyone knows it."

"So what?"

"So from now on I'm going to act drunk every night, and when the time comes to hit the museum, I'll have all these witnesses who saw me staggering around drunk. They'll never suspect me."

"Make sure you just pretend. I'd hate to see you really drunk on the big night."

"Don't worry, I'm not going to touch a drop until it's over."

"What about Frenchy?"

"The same. It's a perfect alibi if we need one."

"You know something, Dirty? Sometimes you actually make sense."

Spring break was extra work, but not as time-consuming as Mike led Patty to believe. Before he started seeing her, he'd let Knuckles take over plenty of times and he'd gone up to Miami for a day or two to get a taste of civilization. Now, though, whenever he saw her he acted overworked and tired and even let slip a couple of times about how noisy the alley was in the daytime with all the kids hanging around it and how he wasn't getting much sleep.

He figured she'd pick up on it and offer him her room to sleep in, which was one step away from moving in entirely, but it didn't happen. She commiserated with him, but no offer was forthcoming. He figured the offer had to come from her, otherwise it might look as though he was trying to move in with her because she had a better apartment than he did, which, because of the housing shortage on the island, was why a lot of people moved in together.

The reason he wanted to move in with her was that he thought he was in love with her. He wasn't positive, because a lot of times in the past he had thought he was in love and then it lasted only a couple of weeks, which in retrospect didn't strike him as love. Or at least love with much of an enduring quality. In fact the last time he had thought he was in love it had lasted only two days. The first day he thought she was sweet and good-natured and great to look at; the second day they went to bed together and he found out she was also extremely selfish.

He thought it would be fun to live with Patty. She liked doing things rather than just sitting around and talking, like most women. Also she wouldn't be hanging around the bar and bugging him all the time, which would be a surefire way to end the romance. Togetherness was fine, but not all the time and certainly not when he was working.

Their sex life, when they managed to find time for it, continued to be great. In fact, if possible, it got better and better. That was why Mike figured when two weeks went by and he hadn't gotten over to her place for more than a few minutes at a time, she'd be ready for any arrangement that would give them some time together.

So, thinking to put the idea in her mind, he stopped by her place during one of the band's breaks on a Monday night. Right away, the first thing she said to him was "Is this a break or an evening?"

He managed to look properly deprived when he said, "Just a break, I'm afraid. There's too much going on over there for me to stay away for long."

"You spend more time with the band than you do with me," Patty claimed, her subtle way of saying he spent more time with the singer. It really cheered him up when she said that.

"You jealous, Patty?" He put his arms around her and she moved in against him.

"No, just lonely."

"Yeah, well, I'm lonely, too. And just to set your mind at rest, I don't even notice the singers these days."

"They've probably been male," she said, which was the truth, but he wasn't going to admit it.

"Even if I was interested in singers anymore, which I'm not, I've been too busy."

"It's hard to believe you live right next door to me and I never see you."

"When I'm not working, I'm sleeping. And I'm not getting much of that, either." He hoped she'd pick up on it this time.

"I'm sleeping, but I'm not getting much work done with all the noise outside."

"Why don't you move your computer in the bedroom?"

"Because it feels like a padded cell in there."

Since his break was almost over, and he obviously wasn't getting anywhere with his subtlety, he compromised and said, "There is one thing we could do," and when she asked what, he said, "I could come over here to sleep. At least we could sleep next to each other, even if we couldn't do anything else."

It was as though a light had turned on behind her eyes. "I wouldn't mind if you woke me up when you came over."

"You wouldn't?"

She shook her head. "And when you got up, we could have brunch together."

So, she was into playing house. He gave her a big smile and a hug. "Sounds great. So why don't you let me have your key now, and tomorrow you can make me a copy."

And then, with the key to her apartment tucked into his pocket, he gave her a kiss that was only a preview of what was to come later.

Mike was whistling when he got back to the Honkytonk. It wasn't exactly moving in, but gradually he'd take some of his clothes over there, and before long you wouldn't be able to tell the difference. And all accomplished without any of those long discussions about "living together" that his friends all went through.

Sometimes strategy really paid off.

IT HAD BEEN EASIER than she'd thought it would be.

Patty didn't know when it had occurred to her that the only way she was going to see much of Mike was to live with him, or even when the idea of living with a man had begun to hold some appeal. She had always liked trying new things, and living with a man would be a new experience.

Roommates had never appealed to her. Communal living sounded awful. Living with Mike, though, sounded rather ideal. Sex was part of it, of course. Sex with him was so glorious that once a month or even once a week wouldn't suffice. Granted, sex would mostly be in the morning when he went to bed, but she had always liked sex in the morning. She was a morning person, not a night person, and often at night she felt more like going to sleep than making love.

Another ideal aspect of living with him would be that he wouldn't be hanging around the house all the time. A man who hung around a lot would drive her crazy. She liked quiet when she worked and she also liked a lot of privacy. But he'd be over at the Honky-tonk and she would have the place to herself.

Also, on the few occasions when the subject had come up with other men, they had always wanted her to move in with them. Moving into someone else's home had never appealed to her. She liked her own furniture, she liked her own taste in pictures on the walls, and she knew that if she moved in to someone else's place she would always feel like a houseguest.

Not that he was actually moving in with her. The arrangement was for him to spend his nights there, that was all. Still, she was sure that eventually he would move some of his things over, which made her glad she had rented a two-bedroom apartment as she had more closet space than she needed.

It was too soon to do it yet, but after a while she'd move her clothes into the second bedroom so she didn't disturb him when she got dressed in the morning, and that way he wouldn't disturb her by coming into her study when she was at work. And eventually they could discuss sharing the rent. Not that she needed the money, but she wouldn't want to feel she was supporting a man.

She had a feeling she was in love with him. She might not have realized it if she had seen more of him lately, but seeing so little of him made her aware of how much she enjoyed being with him and how dull her life seemed nowadays when he wasn't around. She was also crazy about his body.

Patty was too excited to sit still that night. She cleaned her entire apartment, not even minding the blast of music from the Honkytonk. Not that the apartment was dirty, but she didn't want Mike to have any cause to complain. She changed the sheets on the bed, put extra towels out in the bathroom and emptied out one of the shelves in the bathroom cabinet in case he brought along his shaving equipment.

She made room in her closet for whatever he was wearing and made sure there were hangers for him. Then, when she could think of nothing else to do, there was a knock at the door and she thought it was Mike getting off early.

It was only Nacho, though, wanting to use her refrigerator. The electric company had turned off his electricity for nonpayment and she often let him use hers.

"I got a bunch of lobster, Patty. Could I put it in your freezer?" His wheedling tone again.

"Of course," she told him, wanting also to tell him about Mike's plans to sleep at her place from now on. Then her better judgment took over, as she realized it would be pretty tacky to announce it like that. For that matter, she'd prefer keeping it a secret, but that would be an impossibility in the alley.

When he left, she couldn't think of anything else to do so she decided to go to bed. Mike would be waking her up early, and this way she would be well rested.

It was a hectic night, more like a Saturday than a Monday. The college kids, who had been hanging around drinking most of the day because of the dreary weather, were so drunk by ten that the boys were starting fights all over Duval Street, including at the Honkytonk.

Mike had hired an extra bouncer to help Knuckles out, but as fast as the two of them tossed kids, more took their places. The current band—which was rock to bring the kids in—was playing too much Bruce Springsteen, music that always got the kids overemotional, and the cops were being kept busy in the street where kids were walking around with drinks in their hands, which was against the law.

Added to that, the treasure divers had just reached port, and Mike would've loved to talk to them, but they walked in, took one look at the kids and walked back out again. He had heard that the first haul was worth millions.

He had barred Dirty from the establishment for a month because of his fight, but Nacho was there, falling over drunk and trying to hit on the college girls who were having enough trouble just coping with the college boys. He finally told Knuckles to escort Nacho home, saying that he'd do the bouncing while he was gone.

Then Mother Nature decided to have some fun during spring break and, without warning, rain poured down. It looked like about two inches of rain in five minutes, which meant Duval Street was instantly flooded. Cars were stalling, tying up traffic for blocks; kids were belly flopping in the water; others were pushing into the bars even though there wasn't room; hundreds of braless teenage girls in now-soaked T-shirts were causing riots among the boys, and the last straw, the very last—there was the usual power failure.

Thousands of drunk, wet teenagers in total darkness was maybe the worst set of circumstances Mike could think of. The silence didn't even help. At times like that, most bar owners would think of getting in their boats and just sailing off into the sunset. Mike, however, loved a challenge.

He ordered the bartenders to quit serving drinks until the lights went back on, helped the waiters set out candles so he could see what was happening and cursed the advent of the electric guitar. When, twenty minutes later, the lights went on (but only on the other side of the street) all of his customers splashed over there and tried to pile into Sloppy Joe's. Mike cheered them on. He didn't need the business that much, and anyway he doubted whether most of them could even manage another drink.

He got a twenty-minute breather, then all the lights came back on, the band started an extraloud rendition of "Born in the U.S.A." and Mike saw the lemmings heading back for his doors. He had a quick shot of tequila before chaos once more reigned.

It was five in the morning before he was able to grab a quick shower before going over to Patty's. He shaved while he was at it, then found his one remaining pair of clean shorts to put on, and not being able to find a clean shirt, got one from the bar where he sold T-shirts with HONKYTONK on the front of them.

He saw a soaking wet Nacho passed out in Patty's chaise outside her apartment, and decided to leave him there to sleep it off. Inside the apartment, he opened the bedroom door and, in the darkness took off his clothes, put his cigarettes on the night table and got into bed—the wrong side, however, as he landed on top of Patty, who was instantly awake.

"Sorry," he said, getting off her and moving around to the other side of the bed.

The lamp on her side of the bed went on. "Did you have a good night?" she asked, sounding awfully cheerful for having just been awakened from a dead sleep in the middle of the night.

"It rained, or I would've been over sooner," he said.

She moved, so that she was propped up against the headboard. She was looking fully rested, like someone who had already had eight hours sleep. "Oh, good, then my trees got watered."

He was too exhausted even to tell her what a thrill that particular rainstorm had been. "Why don't you turn out that light?" he said to her.

"You want the light out?"

"Yeah, honey, put it out."

Looking a little disappointed, she turned off the lamp, then moved over next to him in the bed, her arm going across his chest. When her hand began to trace patterns on his chest, he realized she was expecting to make love.

That wasn't an unrealistic expectation, of course. He had been looking forward to it also, but now he didn't know if he had the strength even to hug her.

Amazingly enough, after only a few more moves on her part, he found he had the strength after all. His feelings just took over and he knew at that point it had to be love because it wasn't sex at all, he was simply making love to her this time. It was a good feeling.

Feeling somewhat revived, he said, "Hand me my cigarettes, will you?"

There was a silence, then, "I'd appreciate it if you wouldn't smoke in here, Mike."

"I always smoke in here after we make love."

"Yes, but that was different. You were a guest and I thought it would be impolite to ask you not to."

"So what's changed?"

"If there was any ventilation in here I wouldn't complain. You know I never say anything about your smoking. But the windows are covered over and the air conditioner doesn't work on exhaust and a smoky room really bothers me."

Mike couldn't decide whether he wanted sleep or a cigarette more. He was just deciding on sleep when she said, "Why don't we go out in the kitchen and you can have a cigarette while I have a cup of tea."

Making and drinking a cup of tea sounded like it would take a lot longer than he felt like spending on a cigarette, so he said, "Forget it, I don't need one. Let's just get some sleep, okay?"

Patty was already getting out of bed. "I think I'll just stay up."

"Patty, it's six in the morning."

"I don't sleep much later than this anyway. You get a good sleep and I'll see you later. What time do you want me to wake you?"

"Don't wake me. Expect me when you see me."

She leaned over and kissed him. "See you later, then. This is fun, isn't it?"

Mike couldn't figure out whether it was fun or not. But he was sure, if he wasn't so tired, it would be.

DIRTY AND FRENCHY had been in Captain Harry's acting drunk and obnoxious when the blackout occurred. They had immediately raced up to Dirty's apartment and gotten into their disguises. The disguises had been another of Dirty's great ideas.

He'd gotten the idea one night when a couple of hookers had been sitting around his place shooting the bull with him. One had complained about her head sweating, and had reached up and taken off a wig. That had had been a big surprise to Dirty since he had thought the platinum blond hair was her own. Then Cheryl had taken off her wig, and Dirty had made a deal with them.

When he had shown Frenchy the wigs and clothes he had managed to collect from several friends, Frenchy had really gotten into it. Just about every day he would suggest they practice wearing their disguises, and Dirty found himself wondering about Frenchy's enthusiasm. Not that Frenchy made a bad-looking woman. In fact he looked a lot better dressed as a woman than he did as a man. Frenchy even suggested they wear makeup, but Dirty said absolutely no to that.

The problem was he hadn't realized they'd have to put on their disguises in the dark. It was hard enough dressing up like a woman when it was light; in the dark he couldn't tell what he was doing. What had taken them five minutes when they had rehearsed was now taking more than fifteen minutes, but he decided it didn't matter how they looked since no one would see them in the dark. With that in mind, he left the zipper open at the back of his dress. He'd put on a few pounds and now the dress felt like it was strangling him.

When they were finally ready, they cautiously made their way down the stairs to the alley, cautiously because neither of them could walk very well in high heels.

There was a bad moment in the alley when a drunken college kid grabbed hold of Frenchy, mistaking him for a girl, but Frenchy gave the kid a shove that sent him sprawling across the alley, maybe teaching the kid a lesson on how not to come on to girls.

Then Dirty mimicked the kid, saying, "Hey, honey, want to make out in my car?" That broke them both up and they were laughing so hard they could barely walk at all.

Dirty finally took off his heels, suggested Frenchy do the same, and they ran the rest of the way to the museum.

When they got there they had a stroke of luck. The guard must have stepped outside to see if the whole town was blacked out or only the museum, and was standing by the open door. They saw him before he saw them, and they quickly got into their shoes and made sure the guard could hear the distinctive sound of two women walking down the sidewalk.

When Frenchy approached the guard and said, in a high, weird voice, "What happened to all the lights?" the poor guy didn't even have a chance to answer before Dirty took his best shot, then caught the guard as he fell.

He carried him inside the museum, then they both removed their panty hose and tied him up. Dirty used his half-slip to gag him.

They got all the emeralds and about half of the gold. What they hadn't counted on was the weight of the gold; they couldn't carry it all.

When they got back to the alley, the lights were on on the other side of the street and they had to sneak in the back way, over the roofs. They stashed the haul in Nacho's place, then went over to Dirty's and got back into what they had been wearing before. By the time the lights came on in the alley, they were both back in Captain Harry's, acting drunker than ever. They immediately made a nuisance of themselves at the bar and were asked to leave.

Back up in Dirty's apartment, they rolled on the floor laughing. "We did it," Dirty finally managed to say.

"Piece of cake," agreed Frenchy.

"There's only one thing I regret," said Dirty, "and that's not being allowed to tell anyone. There're people in this town who wouldn't've believed I could pull off something like this."

Frenchy said, "I wouldn't've believed it."

Dirty stopped laughing. "Then why'd you go in with me?"

"Why not?"

Dirty started laughing again. "Yeah, why the hell not? Hey, it's all over. Why not really get drunk? This calls for a celebration, right? And if we end up in jail for drunk and disorderly, that's an even better alibi."

"Sounds good to me," said Frenchy.

Chapter Ten

It was one in the afternoon before Mike stuck his head out the door and said, "Hey, how about if I fix the brunch?" Patty had been shooting baskets with Dirty while Nacho cheered them on from his position on the chaise. Now she saw her two friends exchange knowing looks and sly smiles, and she was embarrassed even though Mike treated it all as normal, telling the two guys to get lost because he was wide awake and starving.

She liked the way he offered to do the cooking, but she had everything all ready to go. "Next time will be your turn," she told him, and ten minutes later she had the omelet made, freshly squeezed orange juice and hot blueberry muffins from the Pier House market. She made instant coffee for Mike, a cup of tea for herself, then joined him at the table.

"Looks good," he said, breaking into the omelet with a fork.

She watched while he took a bite, then waited for his reaction.

"Good. What'd you put in it?"

"Lipton Onion Soup mix."

"Really? Makes a good omelet."

That was enough discussion of her cooking. "Do you have to go right to work?"

"Is it still overcast?"

She nodded.

"Then I have to go right to work. I wish to hell the sun would come out so the kids could go to the beach. Unfortunately, the only two things for them to do down here are get a tan and get drunk."

Someone knocked at the door and Patty opened it to see Knuckles, a shy smile on his face. "Mike here?" he asked her, and she nodded and let him in.

Knuckles was just being offered a cup of coffee by Patty when there was another knock, and this time when Patty answered the door it was the redheaded cop on the beat.

"Hey, Chris," said Mike, "what's up?"

"You didn't hear what went down last night?"

"Hear? I was in the middle of it," Mike told him.

Chris shook his head. "Not the kids, although that was bad enough. The Treasure Exhibit got hit."

"Successfully?" asked Mike.

Chris nodded. "Yeah. Whoever it was tied up the guard and made off with all of the emeralds and about half of the gold. During the blackout, naturally, so he didn't get a good look at them. Said he thought it was two women, but on second thought it might've been men dressed up as women."

"Damn transvestites," said Knuckles.

Chris laughed. "It wasn't transvestites, Knuckles. They'd have sense enough not to dress as women."

There was another knock at the door and Dirty and Nacho let themselves in before Patty could even get to the door. She was serving everyone coffee, and everyone was making himself at home, and she hardly noticed when Mike left to go over to the Honkytonk.

They were all speculating about the burglary and who could've pulled it off, the general consensus being it had to be someone local. Knuckles kept to his transvestite theory, Dirty thought it was an inside job, the cop thought it was probably college kids having fun and Nacho didn't appear to have any ideas. But then Nacho looked pretty hung over.

Patty was trying to think of a polite way to get rid of everyone as she hadn't even taken a shower yet, but it was a good hour before the last ones left. And since she had never been to the Treasure Exhibit, or even heard of it, she wasn't all that interested in the robbery.

Now the Brinks robbery—that one had been interesting.

"Is THE STUFF somewhere safe?" Dirty wanted to know.

Nacho said, "Yeah, where I always keep it."

"I don't like it," said Frenchy. "You can't lock your door, Nacho, and people are going in and out of there all hours of the day and night."

"They're not looking for gold," said Nacho.

"Maybe that's not what they have in mind, but I wouldn't trust any of them not to steal it."

"You're talking about my friends," said Nacho.

Frenchy gave him a look of disgust. "Yeah, and every one of them's done time. Get it out of there, and soon."

"I know where I can put it, good and safe," said Nacho. "Patty lets me use her refrigerator since my electricity was turned off."

"I don't think that's a good idea," said Dirty. "We don't want to get her in trouble."

"But they'll never look there," said Nacho. "That'd be about the last place they'd look. She's one of the few clean people in town."

"I still don't like it," said Dirty.

"You got any better ideas?"

"Let me think on it," said Dirty.

"When do you think you can start fencing it?" said Frenchy.

"I'm going to get in touch with some connections I got in Miami. We're only going to get about thirty percent value, but I figure that'll be enough for us to live on the rest of our lives."

Then the talk once more turned to Mexico.

WHEN NACHO CAME BY that night with a large box in his arms and asked if he could leave it in her refrigerator, Patty said, "That's pretty big, Nacho. It doesn't leave me much room."

Nacho gave her his wide-eyed look and said, "But it's a birthday cake for Dirty."

Feeling mean for having given him an argument, she opened the door to the refrigerator, took a few things off the top shelf and moved them to a lower shelf, then stepped aside while Nacho put the box inside.

Then Nacho wanted to stay and talk, and pretty soon Dirty dropped by, and when Mike came over at eleven he brought the entire band with him plus a case of beer, and Patty ended up not getting to bed until two hours past her bedtime. She had enjoyed herself and the members of the band had been entertaining, but she hoped they wouldn't make a practice of dropping by as she had a schedule to maintain.

AFTER FIVE DAYS of sleeping at Patty's, Mike knew it suited him fine. There were little things that annoyed him, but nothing major, nothing he couldn't live with.

One of the annoyances was not being able to smoke in the bedroom. Also, every time he smoked in the living room, Patty was immediately up and cleaning the ashtray as soon as he had stubbed out a cigarette, making him more aware than he wanted to be of how many he smoked.

Then there was her cooking. The meat loaf with Lipton Onion Soup mix had been fine. As had the omelet. But after chicken with Lipton Onion Soup mix, and pot roast with Lipton Onion Soup mix and even spaghetti with the mix, he thought enough was enough and started urging her to eat with him at the Honkytonk.

"You don't like my cooking?" she asked him, making him immediately back off. He didn't want another argument with her.

"Your cooking's fine," he said, trying to put some enthusiasm into the words.

"You're lying."

"No, I'm not, Patty; I just don't see why you should have to cook for me, especially since I got a chef over there and we can eat for nothing."

"You think I'm a lousy cook."

"I never said that. It's just that I'm beginning to feel like I'm sponging off you."

She gave him a doubting look, then started to laugh.

"What's so funny?"

"You don't have to try not to hurt my feelings, Mike. I've been called the lousiest cook in the world by just about every one of my friends."

He was starting to smile. "You serious?"

She nodded.

"You're not that bad, Patty, it's just that Lipton Onion Soup mix gets monotonous. But don't worry about it; I'm a great cook."

Anyway, who cared about cooking? She had everything else going for her.

Little by little his clothes and personal possessions were making their way from his apartment to hers. For one thing she had more room, and for another, it was more convenient. He figured he'd give it a week, then he'd make the offer to share the rent with her. Or even pay the rent. He didn't want their relationship actually legalized, but he wanted to feel they were really living together.

And it would work out well for him, too, because he could put the bands up in his apartment and save the expense of a guest house. All he'd have to do would be move a few cots in and they'd be happy.

Except for Patty's basketball playing. He'd have to do something about that.

DEAR DEIRDRE,

There is trouble in paradise.

That's kind of an inside joke. Every morning the disk jockey on the local radio station says, "Another beautiful day in paradise." Of course he says it whether it's raining or not.

Anyway, back to the subject. Living with Mike is not working out. You know how I like my privacy. Well, it isn't that Mike's around all that much, but when he is around, so is just about everyone he knows. If it's not the guys working for him it's the band, and if it's not knocking at the door they're on the telephone with him every five minutes. It's about to drive me up the wall.

I love him, damn it, but I don't think I can live with him. It's just like growing up again in a big noisy family, and you know how I felt about that. Well, I couldn't do anything about the size of my family, but I can do something about this.

He's also a slob. Now I know I'm a bit compulsive when it comes to neatness, God knows you've told me often enough, but I do think a grown man could pick his clothes up or not leave wet towels on the bathroom floor. I'm beginning to feel like a housewife and I'm not even married!

I hate to do anything about it, though, because when we are alone, it's better than I ever thought it could be. But I'm going to have to. I really think we'd be better off if he stayed at his place and we just dated. Of course I say this now in the clear light of day; in the middle of the night when I'm in his arms I think anything's worth it.

You really thinking of coming down for a visit? That'd be great. I can't wait for you to meet all my interesting neighbors. They're real characters, but I think you'll like them.

And just think, in a few hours you could be out of the snow and on a beach.

Write soon.

Love,
Patty

IT WAS SUNDAY NIGHT and Mike had told Knuckles if an emergency came along to handle it himself. He also planned on leaving Patty's phone off the hook.

He had moved six cots into his apartment for the band, who were now ensconced in his place; he had a bottle of champagne and two steak dinners to take over to Patty's; and tonight was the night he was going to tell her he wanted to live with her and he'd pay half—or all, if she wanted—of the bills. He figured her to be too independent to want to be supported, but he was going to offer it anyway.

And he had bought a ring for her. Not an engagement ring, nothing like that. It was a gold coin ring he had seen down the street and right away it had made him think of her. He figured it would put a seal on their bargain.

When she opened the door Patty took the dinners from him, then raised an eyebrow at the champagne bottle. "You know I don't drink," she told him.

"I thought maybe later in bed," he said, "but only if you feel like it." He figured she'd be as ready to celebrate by then as he.

She took the bottle and put it in the refrigerator and they sat down to eat. He figured he'd give her until dessert, which was Key lime pie, before springing it on her. But being excited about it, he ate his dinner in about two minutes flat, then had to wait while she slowly finished hers.

After she had served the pie and poured them each coffee, she sat down and before she could even start her pie, he said, "I've been thinking about something, Patty, and I got this idea."

"Is that what the champagne is about?"

"Yeah, I guess. The thing is, I think things are working out real well between us." She looked kind of surprised at that, but he didn't pause to consider what the surprise was about. "What I think we ought to do is, I should move in here—I mean really move in, with all my stuff—and we could split the bills. In fact I wouldn't mind paying the bills myself, only you seem pretty independent so it's up to you."

Patty appeared to be in a mild state of shock.

"I didn't think you'd be that surprised. I mean, it's just like I'm living here now. Only I think things should be more equitable. I feel like I'm taking advantage of you by letting you pay for everything."

"I don't think that's a good idea, Mike."

"Hell, Patty, I can't go on living off a woman."

"I don't mean that part. The problem is, I was going to tell you tonight that it's not working out."

Now he felt that he was in shock. Not working out? He thought things were perfect between them. "I don't get it."

"It's not you, Mike."

"Not me? What else could it be?"

"I just don't want you take it personally."

"How can I not take it personally? I want to live with you and you say it's not working out. How much more personal can you get?"

Patty was calmly eating her Key lime pie as though they were discussing the weather. That was starting to really annoy him. "I like living with you; I like it a lot. What I don't like is the lack of privacy."

"How the hell can you expect to live with someone and still retain your privacy?"

"See, I told you you were taking it personally."

"What do you want to do, live together and never see me?"

"Just calm down, Mike. Eat some of the pie, it's delicious."

He shoved the plate away from him, which hit her plate, which flipped her piece of pie in her lap. It was pretty funny, but neither of them laughed. As she was scooping the pie back up on her plate—in small, messy pieces—she said, "I told you, it's not you. It's all your friends. The only time we're alone together is in bed, and then the damn phone is always ringing for you."

Did she think he liked that? The only reason he had had her move the phone in the bedroom was for emergencies. "Look, Patty, the phone can't be helped, but those guys are my friends. Are you saying my friends aren't welcome here?"

"I just don't like communal living, that's all."

"You some kind of hermit up in Boston? You don't have any friends who drop by?"

"People don't drop by in Boston; they call first or wait for an invitation."

"My friends are always welcome in my home." Hell, he liked a noisy house, always had. Maybe it came from growing up with a bunch of brothers, but he liked to have the guys around.

She finished off the pie and looked up at him. "Yes, but this isn't your home. They disrupt my schedule, prevent me from getting my work done, and we're never alone."

"Is that all or do you have other complaints?" Mike knew he was being sarcastic but he didn't care.

He watched as her mouth took on its stubborn look. "As a matter of fact, that isn't all. I'm also pretty tired of cleaning up after you."

"You saying I'm a slob?"

"You said it, not me."

"Okay, maybe I'm a little sloppy, but I could change. But I'll never be as fanatical as you. That little business of yours where you dump the ashtray every time I put out a cigarette doesn't exactly cheer me up, you know."

"My apartment always smelling of smoke doesn't exactly cheer me up, either. If I wanted to live in a polluted atmosphere, I'd take up smoking myself."

Things were not going as he had planned. In fact they were going so fast in the opposite direction it was making him dizzy. "Okay, okay, so we got a few problems. The bottom line is I love you. And that's not something I say lightly, Patty."

It didn't seem to faze her. "I love you, too, but that's beside the point."

"Beside the point? What're you, crazy? I just told you I love you."

"You want some more coffee?"

"Damn it, Patty, is that all you can say?"

She reached over and took his hand. "I love you, too, Mike, and I don't say that lightly, either. In fact I've never said it to a man before. Well, no, that's not quite the truth. I said it to my high school boyfriend once."

Mike had said it on a number of occasions, but he didn't think he had ever before meant it. "So you love me but you don't want to live with me, is that it?"

She nodded, squeezing his hand at the same time, which made about as much sense to him as the situation. "Well, you could have said something. I already moved the band into my place."

"Without even asking me?"

"I didn't figure you'd say no. Hell, we're good together, you know that."

"Maybe, but I think we'd be even better living apart."

"I was going to spend all night with you; I even told Knuckles not to bother me even if there's an emergency."

"I'm sorry, Mike, but I'm way behind on my software and I'm going to have to finish it tonight."

"Damn it, Patty, I'm finally ready to settle down and you're not only telling me you won't live with me, you don't even want me over for the night!"

"You can sleep over tonight if you want, Mike, but I need a few hours alone to get my work done."

"Thanks a lot. I can sleep over, huh? You're making it sound like a high school slumber party."

"You're the one acting childish, Mike. If you don't want to sleep over, okay, but I really have to get to work now."

Mike wondered if it would do any good to give her the ring, but decided it wouldn't. Later maybe there'd be a time, but this wasn't it.

He got up, remembered the champagne in the refrigerator and opened the door to get it. A box that didn't look as though it contained food was sitting there. "What's in the box?" he asked.

"A birthday cake for Dirty."

"Dirty? Dirty's birthday is in November. I ought to know. He got so drunk in my place that night I had to borrow an extra bouncer from Sloppy Joe's to carry him home."

She shrugged. "Nacho said it was a birthday cake for Dirty."

"Doesn't leave you much room, does it?"

"I don't think he'll leave it there long."

"November's a long way off." Mike was trying to be funny but wasn't getting even a smile out of her. "Listen, why don't I put it in one of our refrigerators. We've got plenty of room."

"Thanks, I'll tell Nacho you have it."

Mike reached in to grab it, and almost fell into the refrigerator from the weight of it. "A cake? This couldn't be a cake, it weighs a ton."

She came over and tried to lift it. "I thought he said a cake, maybe he said a birthday present."

"What kind of birthday present would he be keeping cold?"

"I don't know, Mike. I never ask him what he puts in there."

"You mean he makes a habit of it?"

"His electricity was shut off."

"Patty, if I were you I'd tell Nacho to keep his stuff out of your apartment. God only knows what he stores in there."

"I'm not that naive. If it looked like drugs, I'd tell him no. Mostly it's just lobster he gets from someone."

Mike managed to lift the box. "Well, this sure as hell isn't drugs. Nacho doesn't have *that* kind of money."

Even as he was carrying the box to the door he was expecting her to change her mind, tell him to stay. If she didn't, he wasn't going to show up again that night, even if it meant bunking with the band.

But she didn't. All she did was give him a kiss and open the door for him. "You're not mad at me, are you?" she had the guts to ask.

"I'm still thinking about it," said Mike. It wasn't as flip as it sounded. He was still thinking about it.

DIRTY WENT RUSHING down the stairs, crossed the alley, then took the stairs to Nacho's apartment two at a time. Nacho wasn't home.

Next he checked out Captain Harry's and the Honkytonk, before heading down the block to The Bull. And there, upstairs, was Nacho, about two swallows away from being falling-off-the-bar-stool drunk.

He shook Nacho on the shoulder, then caught him as he began to topple. "Nacho, can you understand me?"

"Sure, Frenchy," he said with slurred words.

"I'm Dirty, not Frenchy."

Nacho just closed his eyes. As for Frenchy, he was on his bus somewhere and Dirty didn't know how to find him.

He grabbed Nacho under the arms, pulled him off the stool and dragged him into the men's room. Holding Nacho's face down in the sink, Dirty turned on the cold water and started splashing it on Nacho's head.

Gradually Nacho began to revive. The first thing he did was mutter a few choice obscenities. The second thing he did was pull up his head and try to punch out Dirty. Dirty grabbed his fists and held them tightly. "Knock it off, Nacho. Sober up, this is important."

Nacho blinked bloodshot eyes. "Dirty? What the hell are you trying to do to me?"

"Save your life, man, that's what I'm trying to do."

Nacho tried to take a step and staggered. "I need a drink."

"That's the last thing you need. Come on, let's go down to the Charcoal Hut and get some coffee. I'm buying." Well, not exactly buying, but he could put it on his tab down there.

Four cups of coffee later his words began to make sense to Nacho. "Mike had it?"

"Yeah, I saw him leaving her apartment. He was having a lot of trouble carrying it, too."

"I know what you mean. So what's the problem? We get it back from Mike, that's all."

"What'd you tell Patty was in it?"

Nacho thought about it a minute, then said, "A birthday cake for you."

"Well, if she told Mike that, we're in for it. He knows when my birthday is. I got drunk in his place."

Nacho stood up. "Look, let's just go over to Patty's and ask for the box."

"I think we ought to get out of town."

"No way. That's our fortune in there, our life in Mexico. If they were on to us, Dirty, there'd have been cops at The Bull."

Dirty let himself be persuaded. Anyway, where could they run to with no money? And running away would make them look guilty as hell.

As far as that went, he and Frenchy could claim Nacho was the one who pulled the job. It'd be their word against his.

He was reassured when they saw Patty.

"Mike's putting it in his refrigerator for you, Nacho," she said. "I really didn't have the room for it and he did." But then she added, "He said it wasn't Dirty's birthday, though—that it was in November."

"I can explain that," Dirty told her. "I was adopted, and I celebrate my real birthday and also the day I was adopted. This is my adoption birthday."

Nacho was looking at him like he was crazy, but Patty seemed to buy it. "Well, happy adoption day," she told him, then said she had to get back to work.

"Adoption day?" Nacho said when they were back at Dirty's apartment.

"It's true, you know, I was adopted."

"Adoption day?"

"I had to say something, didn't I?"

"I think we ought to go over now and get it back."

Dirty shook his head. "That might look suspicious to Mike. I'll tell you, Nacho, I think we ought to leave it there for the time being. We're all going to be under suspicion, but not Mike. Those refrigerators he's got over there are so big it won't even be noticed. Wait'll you get it set up, then we'll go get it."

Nacho was looking impressed. "Your mind's really been working lately, you know that?"

Dirty grinned. "You noticed? I think it's because I haven't been drinking as much beer."

"Well, keep off it till we get to Mexico."

"I intend to. But Mexico, Nacho! You know what you can get in Mexico?"

Nacho shook his head.

"Cerveza, man, what did you think? The best damn beer in the world."

Dirty could hardly wait.

Chapter Eleven

Mike was depressed. Sleeping with the band was no party. First, they were all wired at the end of their work and wanted to go out and party. Second, they always had a contingent of groupies who came back with them, and voyeurism wasn't one of Mike's proclivities. He ended up sleeping two nights in a sleeping bag on the bandstand, and by the third night was thinking of checking into a hotel. Then he got lucky.

His friend Kenny, who had a house on Big Coppit, just happened to come into the bar and tell him he was on his way to Tennessee for a month and wanted to stop in and say goodbye.

"Anyone staying in your house?" he asked Kenny.

"No, but if you know of anyone who wants to house-sit, I'd be interested. With the rain we've been having I'm not too worried, but if it stops, I need someone to water the plants."

"I'd like to house-sit," Mike told him.

"You? What about your place upstairs?"

"It's a long story, Kenny. Suffice it to say, the band's now in residence there."

Kenny gave him the key, and later that night Mike packed a bag, rented a car and went out to Big Coppit.

PATTY WAS WORKING HARD, but not too hard to notice that Mike was avoiding her. She wasn't worried. He had said he loved her and she believed him. Still, when her software program was completed and the disk was in the mail to the company who had commissioned her to do it, she stopped by the Honkytonk to see him.

He was tending the downstairs bar and looked happy to see her. "How've you been?" he asked, sounding friendly enough, but not as intimate as she would have liked.

"Working hard, but I'm finally done. Now I can relax and make up a game or two for fun."

"That's your idea of relaxing?"

"That and a few other things."

He grinned. "I've been getting some good sleep lately."

"You noticed, huh? Well, it was only temporary. I'll be resuming basketball practice tomorrow." She hoped he'd say in that case he'd come over for the night.

Instead he laughed. "I'm sure the band appreciated it, but I've been staying at a friend's house on Big Coppit."

"What's that?"

"One of the smaller Keys. His place is nice, right on the water. Want to come out and see it?"

Patty didn't even have to think about it. "Why don't you come over to my place instead? I'd rather be alone with you."

"You will be. My friend's away."

"It sounds good," she told him. "Tonight?"

"Sorry, if only I'd known sooner, I could've arranged something. Anyway, you ought to have more than a night there. Why don't I pick you up Sunday and we'll spend the day and night together? Maybe even do some snorkeling."

Patty didn't feel like waiting until Sunday, but on the other hand, if he wasn't acting eager, she wasn't going to, either. "Sunday's fine," she told him, then, miffed that it couldn't be sooner, she left the bar and went home.

FRENCHY WAS CRUISING down Duval in his new Datsun 300ZX, black with real leather seats. He cruised it three times before he spotted Dirty on the upstairs porch of The Bull. Dirty was looking over the railing at him, gesturing. And the kind of gestures Dirty was using weren't friendly.

Frenchy came to a stop, holding up traffic. "Hey, Dirty," he yelled up at him, but now Dirty was just standing there with his mouth hanging open.

Frenchy figured he'd better give Dirty some story about the car. He turned on Caroline and found a parking space, then took his time walking back to The Bull.

By this time Dirty was out in front waiting for him. "You better start explaining that car," said Dirty, trying to threaten him.

Frenchy gave him an easy smile. "Don't get all heated up; I sold my bus, that's all. Why not go to Mexico in style?"

"You sold your bus for enough to buy that?"

"I told you that bus was an antique."

Dirty wasn't buying it. "That piece of junk?"

Frenchy stayed cool. "How'd you think I got the car? I haven't come into any inheritance lately."

Dirty was losing his cool. "I think you pocketed a few of those emeralds, dirt bag."

Frenchy didn't mind being accused of stealing, since that was exactly what he had done. But a dirt bag? The biggest dirt bag in town was calling him a dirt bag? "Maybe you'd do something like that, but I'm not that stupid. With the kind of heat that's on around here, I was going to suggest we wait at least six months before getting rid of the stuff."

"Six months? Hell, in six months I could be back in jail," said Dirty.

Frenchy shrugged. "It's just a suggestion. Where is the stuff, anyway?"

Dirty looked edgy. "In a safe place."

"Like where? I just hope it's not in Nacho's apartment."

"Don't worry about it, we got it on ice."

Frenchy folded his arms. "Listen, man, I think I'm entitled to know. I mean, you guys might be trying to pull something on me for all I know."

"Yeah, well, if you'd stuck around, you would've known."

"Look, Dirty, I don't want to give you a hard time, but if you and Nacho should get picked up, I ought to know where it is."

"If we get picked up you'll be right with us."

That wasn't music to his ears, but no more than he'd expected from them. Honor among criminals had obviously never occurred to them. "The paper's hinting it's an inside job."

"Yeah, but we know it wasn't, so the cops'll come to the same conclusion soon enough."

"Well, I'll tell you, Dirty. Either you tell me right now where the stuff is, or I might drop a few hints in the right places, if you know what I mean."

"I'm not holding out on you. It's in one of the refrigerators over at the Honkytonk. Mike thinks it's a birthday cake, if he even remembers it's there."

Frenchy was pleasantly surprised to find they were more ingenious than he had thought them. "Not bad," he said, then saw Dirty relax. "Want to go for a ride in my car?"

Dirty shook his head. "Another time. There's a sucker upstairs I wanna hustle."

Frenchy took off, thinking he'd better get his bus off the Key before Dirty or Nacho spotted it. They didn't often get off Duval Street, but you never knew.

He wished he could sell the bus. Not that it'd bring enough for a Datsun, but he was getting short of cash. The only problem was, the woman who bought him the bus put the title in both their names, and she retained the title. He'd be a little smarter the next time.

"HE GOES, 'I sold my bus to get it,'" Dirty was telling Nacho.

"You believe him?"

"Hell, no. I think he took some of the emeralds." Since Dirty had found it easy enough to pocket a few in the dark, he figured Frenchy had done the same thing.

"I don't care so much for that," said Nacho, "but there're a lot of people who're going to be suspicious seeing him driving around in that."

"They'll just figure he found another rich woman."

"Maybe. I just better not see you one of these days walking around with an emerald in your ear."

"Me? You think I'd cheat you, Nacho?"

"Like a shot." Nacho had lifted a few himself before taking the box over to Patty. He was going to be smart, though. He was going to wait until he got to Mexico to sell them.

"I never liked Frenchy," said Dirty.

"So what?"

"I was thinking. Maybe we ought to finger him, then take off to Mexico while they've got him locked up."

"Forget it. He'd squeal on us faster than a stuck pig."

"Yeah, I guess."

"I don't guess, I know."

"Still, it'd be sweet to cut him out. I never could stand Frenchy."

"Sometimes I wonder how you talk about me when I'm not around."

Dirty's face became deceptively innocent, which was a feat in itself. "Hey, Nacho, you're my buddy, you know that."

Nacho didn't believe him, but it didn't matter. Once in Mexico, he'd be the only one who spoke the language. He was sure he'd be able to induce some of his compatriots to relieve Dirty and Frenchy of their shares.

The only problem was, they probably had similar thoughts.

MIKE WAS MISSING PATTY. He knew she had been annoyed that he didn't want to see her until Sunday, but he thought she deserved to be kept waiting.

He still couldn't believe she had thrown him out like that. He had thought it would work. He thought they had a lot going for them. Instead, she gave him some song and dance about being a slob and about never being alone with him.

Well, maybe she'd like life on Big Coppit better. At least it was quiet out there and there were not many people around. And it was far enough away so that friends from the Honkytonk wouldn't just drop by. He'd been thinking along the lines of buying some property out there one of these days; maybe she'd want to go in on it with him.

Yeah, not a bad idea. They could get some land on the water where he could keep his boat docked, build a house, the kind built on stilts, decks all around. Yeah, and maybe he was losing his mind, too. You didn't just buy a house with a woman unless you married her, did you?

Well, why the hell not? He wanted to live with her, and living with her wasn't much different from being married. At least he didn't think it was. He could make some changes in his life. He could get in a manager to run the Honkytonk for him part of the time, take some of the responsibility off him. Hell, he could even work regular hours if he felt like it. Patty'd have the days to herself to do her work, and at night they'd have some time together. He'd even be able to sleep regular hours.

The only problem was it sounded a little boring. It sounded the way normal people lived. He wasn't sure he wanted to live all that normally. With Patty, though, it might be worth a try. And if she didn't like the way he threw his clothes around, they could hire someone to clean up the place. They both made money; that wouldn't be a problem.

She'd probably be glad to get out of the alley. She wasn't the type to live there in the first place. In fact, he was surprised she had lasted there as long as she had. He'd introduce her to some friends of his, people with real jobs, not the kind of characters you found hanging around the alley.

Yeah, maybe it was time he settled down. He was getting a little tired of working all hours, having to contend with drunks and the vagaries of bands and singers.... Well, the singers hadn't been all that hard to take, but life was a hell of a lot more stimulating with Patty.

Marriage sounded rather drastic, but he was kind of looking forward to the reactions he'd get from his friends. They figured he'd never settle down. First, though, he'd see how the weekend went. They'd spend the day on the water, then at night he'd cook for her, show her there was such a thing as food without Lipton Onion Soup mix. Maybe he could even get her to taste a little champagne. They would make love with the sound of the waves outside, then he'd bring up the subject of living on Big Coppit. And see where it went from there.

It gave him something to think about, anyway.

ON THURSDAY NIGHT, Patty got a phone call from Deirdre. She thought it was Mike calling and leaped for the phone, but was just as happy to hear from her friend.

"How's the weather up there?" she asked Deirdre, rubbing it in a little.

"Dreadful. The temperature's breaking all records. And the snow! You wouldn't believe the snow,

Patty. I can't even tell which car is mine out in front, they've been buried for a week. Which is one of the reasons I'm calling."

"You called me to tell me about the weather?"

There was a chuckle. "Hardly. I'm calling to tell you I'm arriving tomorrow."

"Arriving here?"

"Absolutely. You make Key West sound fascinating and my boss has given me a week off. So, can you put me up?"

Patty thought of the extra room in her apartment. And since her own bedroom was soundproofed, Mike would be able to spend the night if he wanted and they'd still have privacy. She hoped Deirdre wouldn't mind the noise. "Of course I can. I can't wait to see you."

"So how's the romance going? Judging by your letters, it's off-again, on-again."

"The romance is on; living together is off."

"I didn't even know about that. You mean you finally let a guy move in with you? What happened?"

"My letter will probably arrive after you leave."

"Come on, give."

"It just didn't work out, that's all. I'll tell you all about it when I see you."

"I could use a little romance myself." She sounded wistful, which was unusual for Deirdre. "I'm expecting you to introduce me to some men, Patty."

Patty thought of Dirty and Nacho and Knuckles, then decided Mike would probably know some men who were more to Deirdre's taste. "The place is full of men and you're coming down at just the right time. I've finished my work and don't have another assignment yet."

"Good, 'cause I feel like partying."

"All you'll have to do is walk out my door."

"So what do you wear down there?"

"About the same as on Cape Cod. Very informal. Pack lightly, we can share."

After she hung up, Patty realized what she had been missing. A female friend. Most particularly Deirdre. She had shared her thoughts with Deirdre for so long, and letters just weren't the same.

Maybe Deirdre could give her some advice about Mike. Deirdre had a better track record with men than she did, even one live-in relationship that had lasted six years. It could be because Deirdre went for more than looks in a man, but Patty felt she was going for more than looks with Mike.

Not that it hadn't been his looks that attracted her first, but it was far more than that now. It was his devious mind in part, but also his sense of humor and the way he was just naturally affectionate with her. And she didn't mean sex, either.

She couldn't wait for Deirdre to meet him. She valued Deirdre's opinion, and she was sure she would like Mike.

PATTY SAW HER FRIEND get off the plane, spot Patty behind the railing of the PBA terminal and fling open her coat like a flasher. Beneath the tweed she was wearing shorts and a tank top. With her thick blond braid almost to her waist, her angelic face and bright blue eyes, her skin already lightly tanned, no doubt from a tanning salon, she looked ready to take Key West by storm.

Patty ran to her and they hugged. Both smiling, they waited for Deirdre's bag, and got a taxi out in front. Then, as soon as the cab swung out on the highway and the water and palm trees came into view, Deirdre said, "This is my kind of place."

Patty relaxed and smiled. "I knew you'd like it."

"What I can't figure out," said Deirdre, "is why my family is from Boston. I should have been born in the tropics; I feel an instant affinity for them."

Patty laughed out loud. "Maybe in a former life you lived on some tropical island."

Deirdre eyed her suspiciously. "Are you making fun of me?"

"Deirdre, you said the same thing when we went to Paris. And Athens. And if I remember correctly, you thought you remembered living in Copenhagen in another time. Actually, I've always thought you were very Boston."

Deirdre allowed herself a brief smile. "All right, so I get carried away. Still, the heat feels marvelous."

"My air conditioning feels marvelous, too."

Deirdre was shaking her head. "No, that isn't how you're supposed to live in the tropics. You should have ceiling fans and wicker furniture and sip mint juleps.''

''That's the South.''

''So is this, my friend. Anyway, I can't wait to see Alyce's Alley. Were you embroidering or is it really as colorful as you make it sound?''

''Probably more so. Also a bit sleazy.''

''Terrific. I love a little sleaze.''

''I like your tan.''

Deirdre grinned. ''Couldn't come down here stark white, could I? Anyway, my health club put in one of those tanning machines; everyone's using them. You get on the bus in the morning and half the people look like they're just back from Florida.''

When the taxi got to Alyce's Alley and Deirdre stepped out of it, Patty saw heads swiveling on the Honkytonk's front porch. Dirty and Nacho, standing sentinel in the entrance to the alley, were both looking bug-eyed.

''Decidely quaint,'' said Deirdre, glancing around the street. ''I think I'm going to like it here.''

Patty introduced her to Dirty and Nacho, both of whom seemed incapable of speech, then took her upstairs to her apartment.

Deirdre gave it one brief glance. ''It looks just like your Boston apartment.''

''I told you I was bringing my furniture down.''

''I would've done it in rattan. And by the way, those characters you just introduced me to, what's their story?''

"They're my neighbors. I told you about them."

"You didn't tell me they looked like they just broke out of prison."

"They're nice, Deirdre; good friends of mine."

"You always were a lousy judge of character."

Not wanting to get into an argument, Patty said, "Come on, just dump your stuff. I want to introduce you to Mike."

"The slob who likes communal living?" asked Deirdre with a gleam in her eyes. "I got your letter right before I left."

"True enough, but he does have his moments." Which moments, she'd tell Deirdre about later.

Patty was used to being totally ignored by the majority of men when she was with Deirdre, and walking into the Honkytonk with her was no exception. She even saw Mike do a double take, which annoyed her but she refused to show it. She took Deirdre to the end of the bar where Mike finally noticed her, and introduced them.

"Deirdre's staying with me for a week," she said.

"Can I buy you a drink?" asked Mike. "Or are you like Patty?"

"I'm not like Patty at all and I'll have a margarita if you make them."

Patty sat and watched as Deirdre mesmerized Mike and every other guy at the bar. But just when she was getting more than slightly annoyed, Mike came around the bar and took the seat beside her. "I've missed you," he said, putting his arm around her shoulders.

She leaned into him. "Then why aren't you seeing me until Sunday?"

He shook with silent laughter. "Can't wait to see me, huh?"

"I'll manage. I'll be showing Deirdre the town."

"Bring her along on Sunday if you want. The house has plenty of room."

That was the last thing Patty wanted to do. Sunday she wanted time alone with him. "By then we'll need a rest from each other."

"Good. I've got a great day planned."

"If you're talking about snorkeling—"

"Don't worry, I'll use Kenny's boat. It has a ladder on it."

"What I want to see," Deirdre interrupted, "is sunset at Mallory Square. It was written up in some magazine I read."

"I've never been there," said Patty.

"If I'd known that, I would've taken you," said Mike. "It's one of our tourist attractions."

Patty thought there were too many tourists on Duval to go looking for others.

"I THINK I'm in love," said Dirty.

"She looks like some movie star," said Nacho.

Dirty wasn't paying attention to him. "You think she'd run away to Mexico with me? I could settle down with a woman like that."

"Forget it, Dirty. If she's a friend of Patty's, then she has class. And no woman with class is going to go with you."

"But I'll be rich."

"Rich has nothing to do with class. Hell, you don't even know how to act around a lady. You think whistling at them and going, 'You ready yet, baby?' shows class?"

"It works, doesn't it?"

"Yeah, if you've got the money to pay them."

Dirty came back down to earth a little. "Maybe I'll get a haircut."

"You'll need a lot more than a haircut."

"Plastic surgery?"

"That'd be a start."

"I think you're full of it. I think you just want her for yourself."

"Not me; I'm going to get me a Mexican lady." Of course, if she was interested, he sure wouldn't turn her down.

SUNSET AT MALLORY SQUARE consisted of aging hippies selling jewelry and T-shirts and cookies and a few other things, while people stood around, waited for the sun to set, then applauded when it did. Patty thought the whole thing tacky.

Not so Deirdre. Her friend was growing more enthusiastic by the moment. She spotted the T-shirts for sale and said, "I could make better designs than those." Patty knew that was true; Deirdre was pretty artistic.

When they got to some paintings of conch houses, Deirdre said, "I can paint better than that." Which was also true. Patty had a couple of Deirdre's paintings in her living room and thought they were excellent.

When they got to Frenchy, who was playing his guitar and singing some god-awful tune, and Deirdre said, "I can play the guitar better than that," she was overheard, and Patty watched with delight as Frenchy stopped singing and handed his guitar to her.

Five minutes later, though, when Deirdre's playing and singing had attracted a crowd, and people were actually putting money in Frenchy's hat, which was now at Deirdre's feet, Patty could see that Frenchy was angry.

He snatched back his guitar to the boos of the crowd, and Patty led Deirdre away.

"Did you see that?" Deirdre was saying to Patty. "I could make a living down here. It would sure beat getting up and taking the subway every day. And slipping on ice."

"They don't make enough to live on," said Patty.

"They must or they wouldn't be doing it."

"It's expensive living down here, much more so than Boston. Like that guy whose guitar you were playing; he lives on some old bus he owns."

"Yeah, but he can't play and I can. I could have paintings, T-shirts and play the guitar."

"Give it a few days, Deirdre. You have the Key West fever, but it's bound to pass."

Later, when Deirdre insisted on going to both Captain Harry's and to the Honkytonk to listen to the bands, and both times talked the bands into letting her sing with them, Patty could tell that her friend was truly hooked. She'd never seen Deirdre enjoy herself so much in Boston.

That was great. Patty liked Key West herself, and it would be terrific to have her best friend living there.

MIKE WAS PRETTY SURPRISED when he saw Patty and Deirdre upstairs at the Honkytonk. It was the first time Patty had ever shown up.

He found a table for them and when the band took a break, introduced the musicians to the women. Deirdre instantly launched into a conversation with them, and the upshot was the band let her sing a couple of tunes. Since the singer this week was a guy, there was no trouble.

When Deirdre was singing a slow tune, Mike asked Patty to dance. He thought maybe she'd say no, but she got up and put her arms around him, moving in so close that what they were doing didn't resemble dancing much.

"I like your friend," he said to her, but saying it softly in her ear in case she took offense.

"I'm glad," she said. "I think she might move down here."

"In with you?" he asked, hoping Deirdre wouldn't mess up his plans.

"No, we couldn't live together. But it'll be nice to have her around."

Then he quit talking and just held her close, thinking Sunday night seemed a long way off.

DEIRDRE, AFTER LISTENING to the noise level in the guest room, opted to share Patty's bed with her. When they were both under the covers, settling down, Patty said, "Well? What do you think of him?"

"If you're referring to Mike, I think he's great. I just hope you don't screw things up with him."

"I think in time we'll be able to work things out."

"Just don't wait too long. I don't imagine he has much trouble getting women."

"That's not exactly what I want to hear, Deirdre."

"Just don't be your usual stubborn self, that's all I'm saying. Listen, I think he's lucky to get you."

"That's more like it," said Patty.

Chapter Twelve

Patty felt as though she could reach out and touch the silence on Big Coppit. Kenny's house was in a setting with water on two sides and an acre of trees on the other sides. She could hear the gentle lapping of the water against the dock, the occasional sound of a bird and that was all.

Mike, wearing nothing but cutoffs, was watching her. "It's nice, isn't it?"

She nodded her head, hating to speak and invade the silence. Something about the setting, the place, made her feel relaxed. She didn't even feel like snorkeling; what she really felt like doing was sitting on the dock and drinking cold lemonade. Just she and Mike, alone with the silence.

Mike put an arm around her and gave her a squeeze. "Not much like the alley, is it?"

"No, it's good to get away for a little while." It had seemed a long wait until Sunday, and now that they were together she wanted to savor every moment of it.

"Come on inside, I'll show you around," he said, taking her hand.

He steered her toward the house and up the stairs. The inside of the house was decorated minimally with rattan furniture and in earth tones. The windows, mostly floor to ceiling, were left uncovered so that from two sides all they saw was the water, and from the other sides it made her feel as though she were in a tree house. A hammock in one corner looked inviting. It seemed as peaceful as the outside had been. Still, she thought a few touches of red would cheer it up.

There was a stereo, but neither made a move to put it on and break the silence. She was about to suggest making some lemonade when he put his arms around her and she knew it wasn't lemonade she wanted.

"It's been too long," he said, his lips brushing her ear.

She moved her head so that their lips met, moving into a slow, unhurried kiss. When his hands slid around her to cup her breasts, and she could feel the beginnings of his arousal pressed against her, she broke off the kiss and said, "Do you really feel like snorkeling?"

His slanted eyes narrowed. "Snorkeling? What's snorkeling?"

Nuzzling his chest with her head, she said, "I don't know about you, but I could use a little nap."

"Nap? You mean as in 'sleep'?"

"Not precisely."

He lifted her chin and looked into her eyes. "What is it precisely you do mean?"

"Oh, precisely. Well, precisely I want to make mad, passionate, endless love with you."

He chuckled. "I can handle the mad and the passionate; endless I'm not so sure about."

"I want it to be endless," she insisted.

"All right, all right, I'll do my best." They were both laughing as she followed him into a bedroom where a ceiling fan brought in fresh air that smelled of saltwater.

"This is the life, isn't it?" he said, and she was thinking how nice it was to be in a bedroom that didn't look like a padded cell, where windows could be left open and no noise invaded the room. Then she stopped thinking at all as he pulled her down on the bed and their bodies took over.

Afterward, and it wasn't precisely endless, he leaned on one elbow as his eyes moved slowly the length of her body. "I love the way you look," he told her.

"So you say. I hear you go for blondes with big boobs."

He made a choking sound. "I suppose I have your neighbors to thank for that."

"It's true, isn't it?"

"In my youth I might have been tempted by the Playboy Bunny type."

"We're not talking about your youth, Enfield; we're talking about just weeks ago."

"I don't know, Patty—I give you a compliment and all I get for it is an argument."

"I can't seem to help it, I love arguing with you. The day you stop arguing with me I'll think you've stopped loving me."

"I think you miss our feud."

"In a way. What's more, I think I could've beat you. I had a few other surprises in store for you."

"As did I. But getting back to your body..." he murmured, one hand now tracing a tickling line between breast and stomach.

"Yes, let's get back to my body."

"I love it. I love the way I can get close to you without feeling like there're two pillows in the way."

She thought about that for a moment. "Are you referring to the fact I'm flat?"

"Not flat; just right."

"I would think pillows would give a sense of comfort."

"If it was comfort I wanted, I wouldn't be with you. Sex with you is exciting, and that's a whole lot more fun."

She grinned up at him. "Want a little more excitement in your life?"

"Give me a break, will you? What's it been, five minutes?"

She looked down at his body and her grin widened. "It looks to me like it's been enough time. Come on, we've only got until tomorrow."

As he moved to straddle her, then entered her with a thrust that seemed to shatter the stillness for a moment, she hoped that tomorrow would never come.

DEIRDRE HAD TURNED DOWN an offer from Dirty to sell her a bike, or even rent it to her for her stay. She found him creepy, the way he kept staring at her, and didn't even want business dealings with him. How Patty could put up with him was beyond her.

She didn't find Nacho much better. When he came by to ask if he could put something in Patty's refrigerator, she took note of the size of the package and told him to forget it. Maybe Patty allowed it, but she didn't want to be caught with drugs on the premises while she was there.

Then she went downstairs to get something to eat and met Eliot, who owned Angelo's Pizza, and he was another story entirely. She took note of his good body, his face that was more suited to a Roman coin than Alyce's Alley and his thriving business, and she invited him out for a drink.

"And risk being torn apart by your neighbors?" he joked with her.

"You mean you're going to let those characters scare you off?"

"I was only kidding," he said. "Come on, you don't want pizza. I'll take you somewhere for some real food."

Over dinner at The Buttery—roast duck that melted in her mouth—he told her about his childhood in New

York. She admired his closeness to his family, liked his attentiveness over dinner.

Over drinks at Louie's Backyard, he told her about the changes in Key West in the past fifteen years. She admired his dark, curly hair, his penetrating eyes.

Walking home, in the moonlight, he told her he was gay. She admired his honesty while regretting the news.

Deirdre decided you couldn't win 'em all.

MIKE PREPARED a shrimp cocktail with his own sauce, cooked Chateaubriand and fresh vegetables and chilled the champagne. The dessert wasn't his own creation, but had been bought at the French bakery. Dinner would be by candlelight.

When Patty didn't demur when he offered her champagne, he figured he had it made.

While they ate dinner he told her he would be content living out his days with her stranded on some tropical island.

"You mean Key West?" she wanted to know, her mind being more literal than romantic.

"I mean any island. I'd be happy with you anywhere."

"I don't know. I think you'd get bored quickly enough on some deserted island."

"Damn it, Patty, I'm trying to be romantic."

She grinned at him. "You're romantic enough in bed; you don't have to be romantic at dinner."

Mike tried again. "All right, I'll be more business-like, then. I was thinking of buying property out here."

He could tell she thought he was just making dinnertime conversation. "I imagine it's a good investment."

"I wasn't thinking in terms of an investment."

"You should when you buy real estate. My accountant's always trying to get me to invest in real estate, says it's the surest thing going these days."

At least that sounded hopeful. "I was thinking of getting an acre on the water."

Patty was nodding. "Waterfront property is always a good bet. Lots of people like to live on the water."

Now was the time to bait the hook. "What I was thinking is, would you want to go in with me?"

He finally had her full, undivided attention. "On property? Is that what you mean?"

He nodded, thinking he had her hooked.

"I don't think so, Mike. First of all, I don't know if it's a good idea to invest with someone else, and second of all, I'd rather invest in something I'd live in."

And now to reel her in. "What I had in mind was getting married and building our own house."

Her eyes widened. "Are you proposing?"

"Of course I'm proposing. You like it out here, don't you? Well, we could get married and live here.

Just think, no more bands at night. Just peace and quiet."

But instead of flinging herself in his arms, as he had been anticipating, she said, "But I love living in the alley."

"Nobody loves living in the alley."

"I do. I mean, it's nice out here for a day, but I'm used to city living. I think I'd be bored to death in the country."

"Obviously you wouldn't like being on a deserted island with me."

"For maybe a weekend. Come on, Mike, you wouldn't really want to live out here, would you?"

"Just tell me what you like so much about the alley."

"I like the people, my neighbors, all the activity. I like having all the stores and restaurants within walking distance."

"You'll get tired of all that."

"Maybe, but I'm not yet. I just moved in, Mike; I don't feel like moving again so soon."

"Damn it, Patty, I'm in love with you, I want to marry you, and you're not cooperating at all."

"Living out here would be all right for you, Mike, because you'd never be here. You'd be at the Honkytonk all the time and I'd be stuck in the middle of nowhere."

He relaxed a little. "No, you wouldn't. I've been thinking I could get a manager in there, maybe work regular hours."

"You'd do that?"

"Why not? You think I like working myself to death?"

She seemed to consider that. "I still think you're rushing things. We haven't known each other very long."

"You think you're going to change your mind about me?"

"No. So what's the rush?"

"I guess it'd take a while to get the land and then for the construction."

"You know what I'd rather do," she said. "Why couldn't we live in my apartment during the week and come out here weekends?"

"You didn't think it worked out when we tried it."

"I like your friends, Mike. If we had privacy on weekends, I could handle it."

"And my sloppiness?"

"I can learn to live with it."

He poured them each more champagne. "Does this mean you'll marry me?"

She smiled. "One of these days."

"Damn it, Patty—"

"Of course I'll marry you. I'd marry you even if you couldn't cook this well. We'll have a wedding in the alley."

Like hell they would—but he wouldn't start an argument now. This one had to be reeled in slowly, inch by inch.

THE DAY AND EVENING had been magical. She had finally worn him out, though, and he was now asleep beside her.

Patty was too excited to sleep. She always got excited about changes in her life, and usually liked to make lists. Well, these changes were going to require a lot of lists.

The marriage, first of all. Saying she wanted to be married in the alley was one thing; trying to accomplish it without her family disowning her would be another. If she wanted to avoid an invasion in the alley by her Irish family and relatives, she would have to be married in Boston.

That would probably be easier on Mike.

On the other hand, he had a big family of his own.

No, she wanted to be married in the alley. Knuckles could be the best man and Deirdre could be the maid of honor and Dirty and Nacho could be . . . well, she didn't know exactly what they could be, but she wanted them in the wedding.

Maybe it would be easier not to tell her family until it was over and done with. Her mother would be so relieved she was married she might not make a fuss. And at Christmas they could go up to Boston and he could meet her family. Christmas in Boston sounded better than Christmas in Key West. She wondered whether people strung Christmas lights on palm trees. Except that when it came right down to it, she wanted her family there, wanted them to get to know Mike.

She wasn't crazy about the idea of a house on Big Coppit, but if it was only used for weekends it wouldn't be too bad. She knew Mike didn't understand how much she loved the alley. Noise and all, it made her feel alive. She wasn't ready for the suburbs; she wasn't nearly ready for rural living, which was what it felt like where they were.

But she was ready for Mike and marriage, and if it was necessary, she was also ready to compromise.

DIRTY WAS IN THE HONKYTONK when it happened. He was sitting at the bar, not too drunk, not too sober, when Bobby Knuckles came charging out of the kitchen. Knuckles charging was something to see.

He watched as Knuckles, clearly upset, consulted with the bartender, and he heard the bartender say, "You better locate Mike."

"What's the matter?" Dirty asked Knuckles.

Knuckles came down the bar and quietly said, "There's this box in the refrigerator, been in there for some time. Anyway, I decided to rearrange the refrigerator and lifted it out, and the whole bottom fell out of it."

Dirty felt the bottom fall out of his stomach but tried not to show it. "Yeah? What was inside, drugs?"

"Worse than that," said Knuckles. "You're not going to believe this, Dirty, but it's filled with gold and emeralds. I think it's the stuff that was stolen from the Treasure Exhibit."

Dirty tried to look properly surprised. "What would it be doing in Mike's refrigerator?"

Knuckles shrugged. "Beats me. Here he is having a romantic night with Patty out on Big Coppit, and I'm going to have to call him and tell him this. This is going to mean the police and maybe his liquor license."

"I wouldn't call the police until you talk to Mike," Dirty advised, and was relieved to see Knuckles nod in agreement.

Dirty figured he had about thirty minutes to get rid of the emeralds, alert Nacho and Frenchy and maybe get the hell out of town. Naw, that probably wasn't necessary. If the stuff wasn't found on him, how were they going to prove anything?

Ten minutes later he was knocking at Patty's door. He knew she wasn't home, but her unsuspecting friend would be even better.

When Deirdre opened the door he gave her his friendliest smile. "Hate to bother you," he said, "but I think I left my lighter over here."

"I didn't see it," said Deirdre.

"The last I remember seeing it was when I was over here, sitting on Patty's chaise. Mind if I take a look?"

She looked like she minded a lot, but she let him enter and he walked past her quickly, lifted the cushion to the chaise and deposited the emeralds there. Putting the cushion down, he made a production of looking underneath the chaise.

"Nope, not there," he told her, then saw her look of relief when he headed back to the door. "Thanks, sorry to bother you."

He could hear her put the lock on the door as she closed it behind him.

Next he went by Nacho's. Nacho was passed out in his bed, and Dirty hid the rest of the emeralds around the place before he woke him up. He'd like to do the same to Frenchy, but he didn't know where he was sleeping these days.

NACHO CAME AWAKE with a start. "What the hell you waking me for, Dirty?"

"Knuckles found the box and he's calling Mike. I don't know whether we ought to get out of here or stick around and play innocent."

Play innocent? Was Dirty crazy? "What're you talking about, man? I gave that box to Patty; she'll tell the cops."

"Tell them you never saw it before."

"You think they're going to believe me over her? With my record?"

"Hell, Nacho, you were only the fence. How much time can you get for that?"

"I don't feel like doing any time."

"Say you didn't know what was in the box. Say you were holding it for Frenchy."

"Like he isn't going to talk?"

"Look, I'm not going to stand around here yapping to you all night. I figure we got maybe twenty minutes before Mike shows up and calls the cops. I'm going out to Big Pine and hide out at Charlie's place."

"I'll probably see you out there," said Nacho, then, when Dirty had left, he got the emeralds out of their hiding place. He went by Dirty's, planted them in the toilet tank, then decided to stay in town and brazen it out. He wasn't dumb; he could beat the rap. He'd just say he didn't know the stuff was stolen.

WHEN PATTY WOKE HIM, Mike figured it was for some more entertainment, but then he saw she was holding the phone out to him. "It's Knuckles," she said. "He says it's important."

It better be, he was thinking. He had left Knuckles explicit instructions he wasn't to be disturbed even if the Honkytonk was burning down.

He said, "Mike here," then was starting to give him hell when Knuckles interrupted him.

"You better get back here fast, Mike. There's a box in the refrigerator and it's full of the stuff that was stolen from the Treasure Exhibit."

"Be right there," Mike told him.

He put down the phone and looked at Patty. "That box you had in your refrigerator, the one Nacho left with you?"

She nodded.

"It contains the stuff that was stolen from the Treasure Exhibit."

He watched as her eyes widened. "I don't believe it!"

"You understand, I'm going to have to tell the police where I got it."

"You're going to tell on Nacho?"

"I'm going to say I got it from you. You'll have to tell them where you got it."

Patty's look was imploring. "You can't do that, Mike; he's a friend of yours."

"Friends don't plant stolen goods on you, Patty."

"But they'll never think you did it. Why don't you just say you don't know where it came from?"

"I'm not lying to the police, Patty."

"What'll it hurt?"

"For one thing, I'd lose my liquor license when the truth came out. For another, I'm not into protecting criminals. Anyway, some of those divers are my friends. They're the ones who risked their lives for it, not Nacho."

Patty's mouth assumed its stubborn look. "You do what you have to; I'm not telling them anything."

"Patty, is Nacho really that important to you?"

"He's my friend."

Mike sighed. "For one thing, Nacho's not a thief, he's a fence. Anyway, I remember that night, and Nacho was too drunk to do anything. I had Knuckles escort him home, then later, when I came over to your place, he was passed out on your chaise outside. I'm sure Nacho could make a deal with the cops—finger the thieves and they'll no doubt go easy on him."

"I never thought you'd be a tattletale," said Patty, obviously not convinced.

"We're not in grade school, Patty, and this is more serious than stealing lunch money. I've got a reputation to maintain in this town and those dirt-bag neighbors of yours aren't going to ruin it."

He hadn't convinced her, though, and they dressed and drove back to Key West in silence. He figured she'd come around. At least he hoped to God she'd come around.

Chapter Thirteen

Frenchy had been getting antsy about someone seeing his bus around town, and tonight was the night. He was a little sorry about doing it as the bus had been a home to him, but it wasn't much use to him now that he couldn't sell it.

He waited until the last of the fishermen went home, then drove the bus to the end of White Street Pier, got out and pushed it in the water. Since he had never swum off the bridge, it came as a surprise to him when the bus only sank a couple of feet and then seemed to rest on the bottom in shallow water. There for everyone to see.

Hell, a picture of it might even make the newspapers.

Well, if Nacho or Dirty questioned him about it, he'd just say that the guy who bought it from him must've done it. Neither of them was smart enough to figure out the truth. And at least they didn't know where he was living.

He'd been staying with a navy woman for a couple of weeks now, and it suited him fine. She paid the rent, cooked for him and even bought him model cars that he spent his days putting together. It sure beat trying to make a living out of playing the guitar at sunset, although he still did that just to keep his hand in.

Of course when the stuff was fenced, he'd head out of town without the little navy lady. Not for Mexico. He didn't want anything to do with those two once he got his share. He had more in mind going back to New Orleans and letting his family see how well he was doing. They never thought he'd make anything of himself. Well, he'd have the last laugh on them.

CHRIS O'NEIL was off duty and driving down Roosevelt Boulevard when he spotted the weirdest-looking hitchhiker he had ever seen. He slowed down, partly because hitchhiking was against the law and partly because he wanted a closer look.

He'd be damned if it wasn't Dirty. Dirty in drag.

He reached over and opened the car door, and Dirty was already sliding in and saying "Thanks" in a high-pitched voice, when he recognized Chris. He could see Dirty was trying to decide whether to accept the ride or run for it.

"Hello, pretty lady," said Chris, then almost laughed out loud at the smug look on Dirty's face.

Dirty had shaved off his mustache and the wig and dress didn't look so bad. But the long legs with tattoos all over them and hair all over the tattoos were a dead giveaway.

Chris got the car back up to forty before he said. "I didn't know you went in for drag, Dirty."

Dirty chuckled nervously. "I'm on my way to a costume party, Chris."

"At this hour?"

"I'm a little late, but better late than never, right?"

He knew Dirty had to be up to something, but he couldn't figure out what. It couldn't be drugs. No one dressed in costume to buy or sell drugs. At least he'd never heard of it. "Tell me where to go and I'll drop you off."

Dirty seemed to relax. "Appreciate it. It's over on Seidenberg. Cut through the parking lot of Zayre and I'll show you the shortcut."

Chris was suspicious but unsuspecting when he pulled up in front of the house Dirty indicated. He figured he'd park around the corner and see where Dirty was really headed for, but he never got a chance. He saw Dirty's fist headed straight for his jaw, and then he was out like a light.

WHEN MIKE PULLED UP in front of the Honkytonk and parked in the taxi stand, Patty got out of the car and started into the alley.

"Patty, wait a minute," Mike called to her.

She stopped and turned around. "Do what you have to do," she told him, then headed home.

Deirdre was watching TV when Patty let herself in, but turned it off and said, "What're you doing back so soon? I thought you were spending the night?"

"You want to hear the good news or the bad news?"

Deirdre shook her head. "Just tell me."

Patty sat down and kicked off her shoes. "Well, the good news is we're getting married."

"And the bad news?"

"I don't think I'm speaking to him."

MIKE TOOK ONE LOOK at the gold and jewels Knuckles had left on the floor for fear of smearing fingerprints, then called the police. When the two detectives arrived, he was downing his third shot of tequila, and he offered them a drink, which they refused, before taking them back to the kitchen.

Detective Casaminor, who wasn't a favorite of Mike's, said, "What do you know about this, Enfield?" in a tone of voice that conveyed he thought Mike was involved. Mike wished they had sent someone he could trust. Street talk had it that stolen goods that had been recovered had a habit of disappearing when Casaminor was on the job.

"I don't know anything about it," Mike told him. "I was keeping the box in my refrigerator as a favor to a friend."

"And that friend is?"

Mike saw Knuckles's look of shock when he said, "Her name is Patty McIntosh. She lives next door over the Atari place. She's home now, if it's of any interest to you."

The detectives exchanged looks, then Casaminor said, "I trust you'll stay here until we return."

"I'll stay here," Mike told him.

Casaminor used the phone to get some backup to take the recovered property back to the police station, then left the Honkytonk without another word to Mike.

"I can't believe you fingered Patty," said Knuckles as soon as they had left. "I thought you liked her."

"I not only like her, I'm going to marry her. But she has some notion that the honorable thing to do is protect Nacho. I don't want anything to do with it."

"Nacho? Nacho's no thief. Anyway, the night of the burglary he was dead drunk. And he wasn't faking it, either: I saw him down about twelve rum and Cokes."

"Yeah, but I'd take odds he's fencing it."

"You think maybe Dirty?"

Mike said, "I wouldn't be surprised."

"I didn't think he had the brains for something like that. And the guard said there were two of them."

"Hell, it could be anyone around here," said Mike. "The alley isn't exactly crawling with redeemable characters."

"I wouldn't have thought you'd give them Patty's name, though. That isn't like you, Mike."

"Listen, Knuckles, I not only have my liquor license to consider, but I think she's wrong. Whoever it was that stole the stuff, stole it from friends of ours. If she wants to consider those alley characters friends, that's her lookout."

"Other than that, did you have a good day?"

Mike started to smile. "Yeah, Knuckles, I had a good day. I was hoping to have a good night, too."

"I had to call you."

"I know. It wasn't a complete loss, though. Before the phone call she did agree to marry me."

"You? I never thought you'd get married." Knuckles looked so surprised Mike had to laugh.

"Neither did I, but she's different. I can see spending the rest of my life with her and never getting bored."

"Congratulations, Mike. Can I buy you a drink?"

"You bet you can."

"Hell, Mike, you know what I just thought of? If they get Nacho for this, I won't have a place to sleep."

"Don't worry about it. I'm about to make you my manager, and my old apartment goes with it."

Knuckles was beaming. "Is that the truth? Hell, in that case, I'll let you buy me a drink."

PATTY WAS SURPRISED the police arrived at her door so quickly. Mike sure hadn't wasted any time telling on her. She asked Deirdre to keep quiet and then let them in, avoiding the eyes of the shifty-looking one and concentrating on the other, but it was shifty who spoke.

"I'm Detective Casaminor, ma'am, and this is Detective Murtchison. We have a few questions we'd like to ask you."

"Yes?" said Patty, determined to protect her neighbor.

"Mike Enfield gave us your name as the person who gave him a certain box to hold." He appeared to be waiting for her to say something, and when she didn't, he went on, "We'd like to know where you got the box."

"Aren't you going to read me my rights?"

"We will if necessary. Right now we only want the answers to a few questions."

"I have nothing to say," said Patty.

"If Enfield's involved in this—"

"He's not," interrupted Patty. "He got the box from me and has nothing to do with it."

Casaminor looked at his partner. "Stay outside the door and make sure they don't leave while I go down and get a search warrant, Jeff."

They left, and Patty looked out the window and saw that, indeed, the other cop was standing right outside.

"I don't believe you," said Deirdre. "What're you protecting him for?"

"He's my friend. I'd do the same for you."

"Yes, but I'm not a criminal."

"Mike says he was probably only fencing the stuff. Anyway, how could I continue to live here if I turned my neighbor over to the police?"

"You afraid of him? If that's it, get police protection."

"They're not going to get me or Mike because we're innocent. I'm sure they'll find out who did it, but it's going to be without my help."

"You were the same way when we were kids, and it never got you anywhere then, either."

"I don't care. I don't tell on my friends, and that's it."

DIRTY, WITH AN UNCONSCIOUS Chris O'Neil in the trunk of the car, was headed for Miami. He figured when he got there he'd ditch the car and hitchhike to California. He'd always wanted to see the Pacific Ocean.

His biggest regret was stashing the emeralds at Patty's to implicate her and maybe take the heat off him. Not that he was worried for Patty, but he could've used the emeralds to cash in for some traveling money.

He knew that Nacho would name names, but he figured he'd wait a day or two before doing so. That ought to give Dirty time to put miles between him and Key West. And with the caliber of police down there, it would probably take them a few more days to figure out he'd flown.

He had gotten as far as the Seven Mile Bridge and was taking it at seventy when he saw the flashing light behind him. Still, he wasn't worried. He knew women could always talk officers out of speeding tickets, and he still looked like a woman.

He knew it was against the law to pull over to the side of the bridge, so he continued on, but as soon as he was off the bridge, he pulled over and waited for the cop.

Unfortunately, he was young and good-looking, and the look he turned on Dirty was one of disgust. Even his platinum wig didn't seem to help.

"I'd like to see your driver's license, ma'am," he was told first thing.

Since he didn't have a driver's license, he said, "I left it at home, Officer, but if you'll follow me back, I'll show it to you." He kind of threw his phony boobs around as he said that, but it didn't seem to help.

"I'm afraid I'm going to have to ask you to get out of the car, ma'am."

Dirty got out, then saw the look of disbelief on the officer's face when he towered over him. And he wasn't even wearing the heels, which he had kicked off as soon as he had started driving.

"Wait a minute," the officer was saying, "you don't look like a woman." But then Dirty distinctly heard some pounding from inside the trunk, and the officer heard it, too, because he looked in the direction of the noise. That was all the time Dirty needed. He slugged the officer, debated whether both of them would fit in the trunk, then decided not.

Leaving the officer and the car he had stolen, he got in the police car and started out once more for Miami. At least no one would stop a police car for speeding.

THE DETECTIVES FOUND the emeralds under the cushion of her chaise during the first five minutes of their search. When Detective Casaminor turned to her, the emeralds gleaming in his hand, Patty didn't even blink, but Deirdre blurted out, "Oh, my God, that's what Dirty was doing."

"Dirty?" said Patty.

"Are you referring to Dirty Dick?" the detective asked Deirdre.

Deirdre ignored the detective and said to Patty, "He came over here earlier with some story about dropping his lighter. I saw him lifting that cushion."

Patty was feeling sorry that both her friends were implicated, then what Dirty had done finally dawned on her. "He wanted me to be blamed," she said, almost to herself.

"Don't protect them anymore," Deirdre told her. "They're not worth it, Patty. They've both used you and now you're letting it come between you and Mike. And Mike is perfectly innocent."

But for some reason, Patty still didn't want to tell on them. Let them act dishonorably toward her if they wanted, but she wasn't going to do the same.

There was a knock at the door and Patty, thinking it was Mike, ran to answer it, but to her surprise it was Nacho standing there. "The cops here, Patty?" he asked her, and she stood aside so that he could see them.

But instead of running, as she thought he would do, he walked inside and up to Detective Casaminor. "I imagine you're looking for me," he told him.

"You turning yourself in, Nacho?" Casaminor asked him.

"I'd like to make a deal."

"This ain't no TV show, Nacho; anyway, we already know Dirty did it. What were you, the fence?"

Nacho, his con-man expression in place, said, "I don't talk without a deal."

Deirdre said, "They already know Dirty planted some emeralds in here," ignoring the look she was getting from Patty.

"I don't know nothing about that," said Nacho.

"Well, what I'd like to know," said Deirdre, "is why you got Patty in trouble. What'd she ever do to you?"

Nacho looked at Patty, and for once he looked sincere. "I didn't figure they'd ever look here, Patty. I wouldn't have got you in trouble on purpose, honest."

Patty, who believed him, was glad now she hadn't implicated him. But then Casaminor started reading Nacho his rights, and moments later the detectives left, after warning Patty they'd want to question her further and not to leave town.

"You sure moved into a great place," said Deirdre, after they had left.

"Yes, and I gave Mike a hard time about moving out of here. Damn, that man is always forcing me to apologize."

"I think you do it to yourself."

"I'm still glad I didn't say anything. But Dirty planting the emeralds on me, that was really low. That was playing dirty."

"Which is probably how he got his name," observed Deirdre.

FRENCHY, WHO WAS AT THE BULL having a drink when the news filtered down the street from the Honkytonk, decided to leave town. He stopped by his girlfriend's house long enough to borrow a hundred dollars from her, then headed out of Key West.

Well, it hadn't been a complete loss. He had a new car, a hundred dollars and a couple of emeralds stashed away in his wallet. They'd pick up Dirty and Nacho, because the two of them together didn't have one brain, but they wouldn't get him. At least he hoped they wouldn't. If they did, they'd find out he had a few outstanding warrants from other states. States that didn't have the most up-to-date prisons in the land.

He had just crossed the Seven Mile Bridge when he saw a cop standing in the middle of the street waving him down. It didn't look like a roadblock, and he didn't think they could've gotten on to him so quick, so he slowed down and stopped the car, then backed up to where the cop stood.

"Can I help you, Officer?" he asked in his most ingratiating voice.

The officer asked him to wait a minute, then the next thing he knew, Chris O'Neil was being helped into his car and he suddenly had two passengers. He didn't think Chris had got a look at him, and he sure wouldn't recognize the car, so Frenchy kept his eyes ahead.

The cop he'd stopped for said, "Some crazy guy dressed as a woman just knocked me out and stole my car."

Frenchy instantly surmised it was Dirty. That meant Dirty was ahead of him, and in a cop car to boot. Maybe Nacho ran, too, and there'd be no one to implicate him.

"That must've been quite an experience," said Frenchy, wanting to hear more.

"I just hope the lieutenant believes me."

"He'll believe you," said a voice from the back seat. "That was Dirty Dick and I can testify to that fact."

That meant they'd be looking for Dirty, and when they got him, they'd be looking for Frenchy.

What he should've done when he trashed the bus was fake his own suicide.

If he got the chance, maybe he'd do just that.

"YOU'RE MARCHING right over there and apologize to him," Deirdre was telling her.

"It can wait until morning."

"No, it can't. That's the best man you've ever met and you're acting like such a fool I could kill you."

"You're overdramatizing, Deirdre."

"Like hell I am. Okay, Patty, if you don't go over there, I will. And I'll offer him a little comfort, too."

"You wouldn't dare!"

"Wanna try me?"

"We can go over for a drink, but I'm not promising to apologize. Anyway, I still think I'm right."

"Yeah, some friends. Nacho's probably confessing right now that you did it."

But Patty didn't believe that for a minute.

WHICH IS EXACTLY what Nacho was doing, only it didn't work because perfect prints belonging to Dirty and Frenchy were all over the chunks of gold. The cops weren't even remotely interested in a deal from him. In fact the entire police department was jubilant at the news that three of the biggest troublemakers in town would be off their backs for a few years.

MIKE WAS SITTING at the bar with Knuckles when Patty and Deirdre walked in. She could've sworn they were celebrating, which didn't make sense, because at the moment she couldn't think of one thing that was cause for celebration.

When Mike saw her, he drew her to him with one arm, then said, "Hey, Patty, meet my new manager."

"Congratulations," she said to Knuckles.

"Ditto," said Knuckles. "I hear you two are tying the knot."

Patty breathed a sigh of relief. "I wasn't even sure you'd be speaking to me," she told Mike.

Mike grinned. "You think I'd let a little thing like getting me in trouble with the cops stop me from marrying you? You can't get rid of me that easily."

"It looks like my two bridesmaids are going to be in jail for the wedding," Patty told him, then explained about the cops searching her apartment.

"Did you know anything about this?" Mike asked Knuckles.

"Not me, Mike. I only slept in his bathroom."

"You were right about one thing," Patty told Mike. "This alley is no place to live. I think maybe I'm ready to move to Big Coppit and have some peace and quiet."

"But you will, with those guys gone," said Mike.

"Forget it," said Patty.

"I don't know," said Deirdre. "If Nacho's going to be locked up, I'd like to rent his apartment."

"I could take Dirty's," said Knuckles.

"And the band could keep mine," said Mike. "We'd control the alley."

Patty looked around at them. "I think I detect a conspiracy."

"You're not really ready to settle down, are you, Patty?" asked Deirdre.

"Well . . ."

"We could use the house for weekends, like we talked about," said Mike.

"Well . . ."

"Lots of drug smuggling in and out of Big Coppit," said Knuckles, then got a dirty look from Mike.

"Isn't there any area of the Keys that isn't corrupt?" asked Patty.

"Yeah, Alyce's Alley," said Mike. "At least when we take it over it won't be."

"And we can get married in the alley?"

"Why not?"

"I'll even sing at your wedding," said Deirdre.

"You know something," said Knuckles. "I never thought I'd see the day when Mike would marry a snowbird."

"What's a snowbird?" asked Deirdre.

And while Knuckles was explaining it to her, Patty took Mike by the hand and led him away from the others. "I think I better warn you about my family," she told him.

"They're not going to approve of me, is that it?"

Patty chuckled. "Not approve of you? They'll be so relieved I'm getting married they'd approve of anyone at this point."

"Then what's the problem?"

"I'm just afraid they might overwhelm you, that's all. If you haven't had an experience with a big Irish family, you're in for a shock. My mom will treat you like a long-lost son; my dad will tell you the family history; my sisters will warn you all about my shortcomings, and my brothers will challenge you to arm wrestling."

"Sounds just like my family. We just better not mention to yours that mine is English."

Patty laughed out loud. "On the contrary, I think that's the first thing we should mention. That way they can argue Irish independence and leave us alone."

"You know, Patty, you're making my mother the happiest woman in the world. She's sure I'll never get married."

"Just so I make *you* happy; that's what's important."

"Hell, you already do that."

"So do you."

He put his arms around her and she leaned her head on his shoulder. "I'm just sorry everyone's not as happy as we are. You know what I'm going to do, Mike? I'm going to send those guys cookies in prison."

"Patty!"

"Why not? Despite everything, I still like them."

"It isn't that. I just can't see them appreciating cookies made with Lipton Onion Soup mix."

"Then I'll make them for you."

"I GOT A BOX of cookies from Patty," said Nacho.

Dirty said, "So did I."

"I haven't gotten nothin'," said Frenchy.

"I had this idea," said Dirty.

Frenchy said, "No more of your ideas, Dirty."

"No, I mean it. What I think is we ought to work on Patty, maybe get her to smuggle us in something."

"Like a file?" asked Nacho.

"Yeah, something like that. She likes us, you know? She really likes us."

Nacho shook his head. "Maybe so, but I hear she's marrying Mike. We probably won't even get any cookies anymore."

Dirty's face fell. "Oh, well—jail's not so bad. At least I don't have to clean the alley anymore."

"Yeah," said Nacho, "that was a real hard job."

"I had to get up mornings, didn't I?"

Nacho said, "I can remember the first day she arrived." As he said it, the other inmates moved over to listen.

Patty was already becoming a jailhouse legend.

These two absorbing titles
will be published in May
by

HARLEQUIN
SuperRomance

JUST ONE LOOK by Barbara Kaye

Lisa Canaday's mother was a renowned artist – and she was going blind. Fiercely protective of her mother's remaining time to create, Lisa joined her on secluded St. Angela island.

But Lisa's grandmother was determined to have them leave the island, since she wanted the property for a resort development. Having disowned her daughter many years before, she dispatched charismatic Eric Jarrod to handle the negotiations.

Eric's intrusion did more than shatter their solitude. The passion he stirred in Lisa persuaded her she could love again. But she knew love was all they could ever share . . .

MEANT TO BE by Janice Kaiser

Diana Hillyer's life in Washington was fulfilling and safe – and worlds apart from Honduras.

But that's where she found herself when her dearest friend asked Diana's help in rescuing a teenager who had been forced into prostitution. Within days Diana learned that an American soldier, Cleve Emerson, held the key to the girl's freedom, and that he refused to help.

Diana found his stubbornness infuriating . . . and his allure irresistible. But a soldier's life allowed for only the briefest relationship. Could she accept that they would only have days – possibly hours – together?

Next month's titles

EVER SINCE EVE *Pamela Browning*

Blacklisted by the mill owners in Wrayville, North Carolina, Eve Triopolous had exhausted all conventional options. What Derek and Kelly Lang offered was not precisely a job but more of a service they needed rendered. The money appealed to Eve in her desperation, but more compelling was the desperation she saw in the faces of the Langs.

Eve didn't give herself time to think; there really wasn't a choice to make. So she signed the papers that would bind her to the Langs for at least nine months – the time it would take her to carry their child to term.

MACKENZIE'S LADY *Dallas Schulze*

An innocent quest for a friend's watch took Holly Reynolds to Tijuana. Holly didn't recover the memento, but after being subjected to the horrors of multiple propositions, a bar-room brawl and a dubious rescue by an unsavory character named Mackenzie Donahue, Holly didn't care about the watch – she only wanted to get back to Los Angeles, where she would be safe at last.

But Holly wasn't safe. An unwitting player in a deadly game, Holly was bound to get hurt, one way or another. Mac wanted to prevent that. But would Holly thank him – or hate him – for his interference?

MINOR MIRACLES *Rebecca Flanders*

Michael Bradshaw was certainly unique. His oddly hued eyes lent him a mystical air, a quality that was confirmed by his abilities. For hours the scientists at the Maryland research center watched a demonstration of bizarre, supernatural strength as Michael melted iron chains, boiled water, and caused disconnected telephones to ring – using nothing more than the power of his mind.

As a professional psychologist and part-time parapsychologist Leslie Roarke was trained to seek rational explanations. But when those strange topaz eyes looked up, they somehow saw through her two-way mirror, and smiled knowingly at her, Leslie could only wonder: exactly *what* was Michael Bradshaw?